THE SWINGLES

Case Studies in Variant Sexual Practices

by

CARSON DAVIS

The Borgo Press
An Imprint of Wildside Press

MMVII

CONTENTS

INTRODUCTION

They call them apartments for "single people only", but another word, in many cases, could be "sex-isle".

It is hard to tell for sure how the whole thing originally developed. Possibly because single people have a totally different kind of life than married couples. They want to swing, have parties, live near people with the same interests and same desire to learn what adult life is all about; and/or the ways of the bachelor man and woman.

Some sharp promoter, no doubt, came up with the original idea and it has taken fire, spreading across the nation.

Some of the apartments aren't any different from those offered to married couples, other than the fact nobody really seems to care what kind of parties go on and how long into the night they swing.

There are exceptions, of course.

But most interesting is the fact that many of these mod apartments offer more than merely the private units for young people to live. They can have any one or all of the following features (outside of being fully furnished, air conditioned, dish washers, washing and drying machines): Game rooms, sauna baths, pools, snack bars, delicatessens, drug departments. In fact the most complete ones are islands unto themselves where single people can come home from work and never leave the grounds, other than to go to movies or out-on-the-town. They are self-contained little "cities" where anything can go! And it usually does.

The reason the book of case histories was possible is what a professional author and/or sociologist might call a wild bit of luck.

Normally, in putting a collection of case histories together, it is necessary to compile material from disconnected sources, searching, digging, stacking case history on top of case history until there is enough subject matter on one basic "theme" to put together a book. It can be quite an exhausting job, taking weeks and months to get the last few case histories that will complete and round-out a study.

What happened here was that a friend of mine, male, single and a swinger on his own right, became a manager of one such apartment for "singles only". And it was one of the luxury complexes with over forty units, ranging from singles to two bedroom apartments.

Since his own story turned out to be of some interest, detailing much of the life in this island of pleasure—as he calls it—and revealing something of the activities that go on in such a place, I recorded his story in detail. At first I believed this material would merely serve as background facts to be used in an introduction. As it turned out, what he had to tell involved as much insight and actual description of the types of men and women who live in such places—along with an intimate "confession" of the advantages of managing such an apartment for a swinging bachelor, plus some intriguing revelations about his own private moral code, his psychological make-up—that I was compelled to use the interview as a case history and study of the mod bachelor.

Many people will find this book a little shocking, some will be sorry they didn't have a chance to live in such a pleasure isle when they were single; others will discover themselves intrigued and fascinated by what is happening in the younger generation.

This is a study of what is taking place with the youth of today and it certainly gives a look into what the future might surely be like.

As one young man told me: "This is the scene, man. All of us are just average young singles, not hippies or far-out nuts like that. We're young, unmarried and interested in living to the hilt. And this kind of action is catching flame! I'll bet you a million that what we're now involved in will be the common scene in the future. Maybe people won't even bother getting married—unless they want kids. Society is changing, the cultural needs of each human being is changing the moral attitudes of the world. The future is going to be a totally different place. I'll bet that same million—or another—that it won't be too long before population control will make this kind of living experience the norm for every man and woman. They won't want to get married.

"They'll live together for a time. Or won't even bother with that. Because the way we have things, you can have an all-night sex party with some beauty, get up any time of night or in the morning, leave her pad and walk over to yours. We're almost like one happy community, a kind of tribe-of-old, living in the same building but merely having different private rooms. In other words, man, we can have personal privacy or all the company we desire. It is up to each person. This is the ideal way to live and it won't take long before the world-culture will come to this realization."

I don't know if I agree that it is an ideal form of living; I can say, though, that some of his observations might not be so far off.

Another member of this pleasure island, an attractive young girl said this:

"Some people might think that the new morality is breaking down the family-unit. That there won't be any more marriages in the future if things keep on the way they are. I don't know if that's true, really. Our generation isn't doing much more than our folks' generation did, but we're just being more honest and open about it. They certainly got married. But that's not the issue. Marriage isn't the answer for everybody. If you have marriage you have divorce. People dig each other for a while and then simply get bored with one another. One or both cheat on the other. Or they end up getting divorced.

"As for wanting children—I guess I do. Most women are that way. But there is a time and place. In the meantime I want to live a life that involves relating to men in an honest and total way. And, anyway, in the future the whole thing might be taken out of our hands. The world is overpopulated, anyway. And it's getting worse. What does the future hold? I don't know. I don't think anybody knows. The important thing is to get the most out of life while you can.

"For a single girl or man, this kind of living is great, because it solves the old problem of meeting people your own age, solves the dating-game difficulties. Everybody who lives here feels the same way—we're actually a little city, a kind of unrelated family who knows everybody. Like a small town without the same small town morality. Dig?"

Not every one felt exactly the same way; or at least felt for some reason they didn't want to admit it. Everybody has their own personal hang-ups. But in the kind of apartment these young adults were living there was room for all kinds—and no room for blind hatreds. I met and talked to members of just about every race and color. Everybody was openly accepted as an equal to be judged on what kind of person they were, not what color of skin covered their bodies.

These case histories show what it is like to be young and honestly seeking a fulfilling and rewarding living experience. I'll let the people talk for themselves and the reader come to his own conclusions.

—CARSON DAVIS,
Sherman Oaks, California

THE SWINGLES, BY CARSON DAVIS

CHAPTER ONE

PAUL—MASTER OF PLEASURE ISLAND

He's lean, good-looking, dark-blonde, well-muscled, five feet eleven inches, broad-shouldered, solid-framed. He has been married once, when he was seventeen, divorced at the age of twenty-four. Has worked as a bartender, insurance salesman, agent for rock-and-roll groups, attempted for a short time to make it in acting, done some writing, but gave it up as "too difficult" after selling half a dozen stories to science-fiction and detective magazines, been a "beach bum"—after his divorce—a fry-cook, managed a motel in Santa Barbara, did a few "terrible years" as what he calls "a captive of the United States Army", at which time he was stationed first in New York and then in England. Present interests involve survival, swinging girls willing to be "groovy" in every way. And have the good-life as a bachelor.

I knew him in high-school, was responsible for getting him interested in writing, "suffered" at times over cocktails through his marriage trials. Lost track of him shortly before the divorce; re-established contact after he returned from the service, when we socialized together—since both of us were by that time un-married. We drifted apart socially, but spent an evening together once-in-while to catch up on each other's experiences. In other words,

11

we're long-time friends who can be out of contact for any number of months or years but find little has changed between us when we do meet (other than a bit of aging and a bit more experience in life).

Because of his own experience in writing, I gave him the transcription of our interview, edited down to cut out socializing, so that he could polish up any points he felt important enough to work on. I cut what turned out to be something like twenty-thousand words (a vast expansion on the original material) down to the basic "meat".

Before reading his monologue I feel it would be of some interest to relate a portion of the interview which was not included in this material.

We came together for some social drinking and conversation one night. As a result of what he told me about his new "job" as "master of pleasure island", I stated it would make a great study, if he thought there were enough men and women who might be willing to tell their stories. He promised to look into the matter. And within the week I received a call from Paul saying there were more than enough of the "kids" willing to cooperate to fill several thousand pages. I invited him over and interviewed him on tape in order to get background material before setting up any interviews with the other people. While we had casually covered the subject of the apartment "for singles only" during his first visit, it hadn't been possible to go into anything but general concepts. Once the tape had been spinning a few minutes, half a drink consumed by each of us, Paul said:

"For one thing this is a great swinging arrangement for the single guy—and girl, too!—one could get. I couldn't believe it! It's a dream! Really crazy!"

"I would imagine," I said with a grin in my voice.

"You should move into such a place. The girls are really ready, willing and able to offer a great, mature relationship. No hunting around. No throwing away a couple of bills just trying to get some chick in bed!"

"Sounds great, but it wouldn't work for the kind of life I live. Plus, there's plenty of that kind of thing around for me when I want it."

He chuckled. "Yeah, I see what you mean. After scanning through your case history books...boy, I don't see how you turn down some of that stuff."

"It's not hard."

"If I didn't know better I'd say there's something wrong with you!" he announced, laughing.

"If you saw some of the women, maybe you wouldn't think so."

"Dogs?" he inquired. "You mean you mislead the reader about them?"

"Hardly," I said. "Though, of course, it would be a very cute little commercial move."

"Especially with the ones you admit bedding."

"But it isn't necessary," I said.

"Not every woman is that great or beautiful, surely," he suggested with a knowing wink.

"For one thing, Paul, every woman has a beauty all her own. There are different kinds of beauty."

"Oh, come on, don't give me that kind of cop-out."

"I'm not." I said. "And, in any case, most young women nowadays who are having a swinging life are pretty attractive."

"And they all look the same in the dark; or up-side-down?" he offered, laughing. "Is that it?"

"I didn't mean that, either. The thing is that I *don't* involve myself with these women I interview."

"That's not what you claim in your books."

"I should have said that *as a policy* I don't—as a fact of life it is sometimes not only hard to keep from getting involved but impossible—simply because I'm a human being.

"You see, some women are shy and shaken when talking to me, some are cold-business, considering me nothing more than an extension of the tape-recorder; but there are those who get erotically excited talking about their sex-life and it turns them on. I become an object for their sexual hungers. If, for one reason or another, *I'm* pushed into their seductive moves…pushed beyond control, it happens. At times a case history actually develops because I'm dating a girl, and having an affair with her. Then, at her suggestion, she goes into the 'confession' bit."

Paul chuckled again, then told me: "Some of the girls you'll be interviewing for *this* book will be out to *turn* you on—because they'll want to find out what it is like with you. They won't be hung-up females and they will be so damned sexy that you'll find it impossible to keep from socking it to them! I know. I've made the scene with a few of these groovy chicks that throw it around at any stud willing to bed-down with them. They come on pretty strong, are quite direct about what they want and go right to it without passing go and not worrying about collecting two hundred dollars—only a few hot wild thrills with a man."

"You make it sound rather interesting," I admitted.

"More than interesting. We have quite a crowd. I don't know if it is typical of other places like ours. I believe, at least in part, that the people attracted to this apartment are drawn by the general atmosphere. There's a no-punches held policy. No prudes allowed. No squares. And the information gets around. In other words, word of mouth. A guy or gal might be dating somebody and that person just finally moves in when there's a vacant room. We have quite a waiting list! The owners plan on building more of these apartments because its good business.

"But don't get the idea this is some kind of orgy-house or some degenerate place of sin. They are just normal, red-blooded singles who aren't afraid of a little open sex, who want to live a little before they get married and want to do it in style. And there are a great number of such un-hung people!"

Now to his monologue:

I call it *Pleasure Island*, but it's a self-contained apartment building, built in a huge square, open in the middle for a large pool. It has everything the singles need. We don't have to go out for magazines, booze, certain kinds of food or drugs. It's all in the building. The shops are open to the public, too.

I was pretty surprised about the whole thing when I first learned about it. The owners told me this was their policy:

"We rent to mature, over-twenty-one, adults, single, modern and aware of what is happening. In other words, they are the type of people who like a swinging social life and enjoy the idea of not having to go too far to get it. We don't want prudes.

"You'll have to screen singles who want to rent. Anybody who doesn't fit into the social scene should be given notice to move. If you get complaints about the activities of others, give such a prude the vacate notice. We don't need this kind of thing. We don't want it. If you have somebody who doesn't like the noise, out they go.

"We want people who desire the freedom to live the kind of life they desire without restrictions. We believe there are a lot of people who don't mind putting up with a little noise from others, because they want the right to make with the same kind of action. In other words: they want to have parties and entertain and not be turned off at 10:00 P.M. That's the kind of people we cater to. But no hippies or far-out nuts. No degenerates. Just nice, average, hard working people who like to live it up just as hard when working hours are over."

In simple terms they were saying: Hands off. Let the people live their own lives as long as they are nice, normal single men and women who wished to be left alone and not bugged by others.

What a wonder that was! I didn't think people could be that realistic.

Well the first day I took on the job, moving into the one bedroom apartment allowed the manager, since he would have to use a part of his living room as a kind of office (otherwise they'd have given me a single) I learned very fast how swinging and groovy the place was.

The girl living next door, a dark-haired (in long straight waves), tall female with a stacked figure, wearing slacks and a man's-style shirt (top buttons open to give some kind of evidence that the thrusting points pressing against the cloth weren't padded!) went out of her way to be very friendly. She tried to convince me I should let her help getting my things arranged.

Naturally I refused, but her invitation of a drink once I'd gotten settled was readily accepted. For one thing, she had a great way of using her full, wild lips to the best sensual advantage—several times licking them with the point of her tongue. To say nothing about her flashing dark eyes. She had high cheek-bones and long tapering legs, fully packed at the thighs—and a nicely flat stomach off-set with a slightly swayed back that did great things to accent her molded firm-looking fanny.

I can't say I didn't expect something exciting to happen after the drinks, though in the manner it took place I must admit to a little bit of surprise.

I'm not a square. I've had my mental "black book" filled with a good number of girls willing to share a bed with me.

I've picked women up at bars who were pretty horny about my blunt passes.

I've been approached by prostitutes in this and other countries who came right out and offered any kind of trick I wanted; offers made in hotel lobbies, elevators, on the street and in bars.

Gale—the girl next door—immediately introduced herself upon first seeing me, saying: "You look like some fun—hope you're more groovy than the last manager."

I politely asked, my eyes feasting openly on her figure in the same manner she was giving me the once over: "What was with the last manager?"

"He was all right; and all that. Just didn't make the social scene too much. Oh, a few times. But he wasn't quite the swinger the rest of us are. That's why he was dumped. Hope you have better luck."

Her eyes and smile offered quite a lot. And she twirled the cigarette between her lips like blowing a man's cock. She blew smoke as if throwing a kiss.

Well, tired as I was with the moving and all that, I can't say I wasn't looking forward to a drink with Gale. The suggested promise that she was a highly-charged girl who just might be willing to do more than devour cock-tails, if we hit it off good, did a lot to power my interest in developing a relationship. I wasn't fool enough not to know the score about the apartment and those living there; though I didn't have any idea just how fast and far anybody might go, even with a total stranger.

She had changed by the time I knocked on her apartment door.

She had on a low-cut black cocktail dress that opened to a point well below the bottom of her breasts, making a wide V. The gown had narrow straps over the shoulders. It certainly did something to her voluptuous figure; to say nothing about what it did to me.

I felt tingles twitching all through my cock; just at first sight.

The dress was tight enough to suggest there must be very little under it other than her naked self, and if anything it had to be damned thin. The cloth tapered around her curving hips and came to a stop about six inches above

17

lovely knees. Her flesh was creamy and smooth looking. She didn't wear any nylons, which seemed pretty wild considering the formal dress. She had on high heeled shoes.

Later she told me why the lack of stockings, though it wasn't necessary by that time. I'd guessed the obvious. When a girl is on the make and doesn't like to fool around, the easier she can get undressed, the better. Nylons would have helped to slow things down; and Gale wasn't the kind of girl to creep into bed—she leaped!

We sat on the sofa, a long affair, big enough for a tall person to stretch full length; or seat about five people comfortably. All the apartments are furnished in the same way: modern, flashy-looking furniture—but cheap enough to make sense.

Gale made no effort to keep any distance between us. She let me sit first by simply being busy pouring the martinis into two glasses set on the long coffee table in front of the sofa. Then she slipped around in front of me in such a manner that her legs touched my knees. When this woman sits it is an animal, sensual action, impossible to detail. She is graceful, yet at the same time gives the impression of being a sexy cat-in-heat, kind of squirming all over at once.

I remarked on her dress, saying how attractive it was. The rest of the conversation went something like this—hitting the high spots.

"You like it?" she beamed. Her thigh was just touching mine and the contact was highly erotic.

"Terribly nice to do all that for me," I offered, holding the cocktail glass in my right hand, nervously fingering a cigarette in the other.

"I thought maybe you would think it was a little too daring, but it is one of my favorites. I'm glad you like it. I paid quite a big bill for it—had to have it reworked so it fit my and bust line hugged my body just right. Also had

18

them cut the neck this way. I'm proud of my body."

This frank, honest statement set me back. I didn't know what to say. I sipped my drink instead of making any remark.

She leaned a little closer, as if about to confide to a near and dear friend, and I was enveloped in erotically stimulating perfume. Her face was close enough so that when she spoke I could feel the warm breath of her words.

"To be truthful, Paul, being over twenty-one—well, frankly I'm twenty-six—I've had enough experience in life and men to know the male sex doesn't find me exactly ugly and undesirable. And that gives a girl a kind of security about life and men. I'm not afraid to show-off some of my best features to all men—saving the best of all for only the special ones, naturally—in a proud and open manner.

"A girl who has a beautiful or sexy body shouldn't be cheap with it. After all, you are only young for so long and its best to make the most of it while you have the goods to reveal. Don't you think that's right?"

I couldn't agree more and told her so.

"I mean, Paul, there are a lot of women who secretly think they are God's gift to men, but wouldn't 'think' of admitting it publicly to anybody! I think that's being dishonest. If you have something great why not admit it and let others admire and see. Don't you agree?"

"With that shape of yours, I couldn't agree more," was my very classic line.

"Is it wrong? After all, we're both adults and wise to the ways of our world. It is kind of silly to play childish games with one another. Like when you meet someone that attracts you, there's nothing wrong in letting them know. And there's nothing wrong in making every effort to show yourself off to the best advantage in the hope they will be strongly attracted to you. See what I mean?"

"I can guess, hopefully, that you're implying you think I'm attractive and want to be just as attractive to me, is that right?" I offered, playing the game her way.

"Great!" She leaned away from me, patted her lovely leg in open delight. "I like that! Honesty! Open and above-board."

I couldn't keep my eyes off her breasts. From the side angle it was possible to see the swelling inner and bottom curve of both breasts. Since the back was almost backless, the outside bulge of her breasts was partly revealed. They were firmly and sensually muscled. Well, that's one hell of a way to say it. She was hardly muscled like a man. Just that her breasts were large, fleshy, but firmly formed—and there is such a thing as a breast-muscle even for a woman! The sight was storming up my male juices. I could feel all the excitement gathered up like a tightening knot between my legs. More specifically stated: I was getting one hell of a hard on.

What she said next tingled that erection to fullest length against the tight pants; knotting up my testicles with surging, bubbling pain.

"Paul, I don't believe in playing games with a man I find attractive. It can burn up so much time that could be used in a far better way. I don't bother myself with any man I wouldn't consider exciting to develop a thing with. I hope it isn't shocking to you for me to admit this, but I haven't been a virgin for more years than I like to count and I believe it's silly to play like I don't know the score. Is that too much for you to take all at once?"

"It does cut through a lot of stilted social games, doesn't it?" I offered in a far too husky voice.

She laughed hard at that, and said: "I guess we feel the same way."

"And...how is that?"

"What do you think? Are we going to play games or are we going to relate in a sophisticated and mature way?"

"I'm never against relating to a willingly attractive woman."

"I don't relate to everybody. I relate only to those who hit me right between the legs! On first or second sight. If I see a guy that flips me I don't want to wade through a lot of chatter and meaningless actions. We're going to be living right next door to one another and we might as well get off to a good start. And since I think its great having you as the manager—rather than some unattractive SOB—meaning I was very pleased and surprised when I saw you this morning!—I feel it's best to get things started off in the right way."

"And I would hope your idea of the right way is as promising as it sounds." I simply couldn't bring myself to rush into the honesty "word-game" in quite the speedy fashion as Gale did. I found myself a bit startled by her open frankness and quick action. But groovy! She wasn't going to play games.

"My ideas are pretty simple. I believe that while a person is young and single they should live by their guts, getting as much out of life as possible, no holds barred, no silly games, because we don't know when the chances will be gone."

She leaned closer again, as if confiding: "I went through quite a long period of loneliness after my second divorce. It was hard to meet men interesting enough or willing enough to keep me happy. When I learned about this place I decided it was just made for a girl like me. I don't want the marriage-scene and I'm not interested in anything serious with a man. Not in an emotional way. I want to relate completely to those guys that offer the good times. I don't ever want to be lonely again. And I'm not! Not here."

"I take it you must be pretty popular around here," I observed.

"Popular enough to have my pick of at least some guy every night, if I want to."

"I'm lucky you weren't tied up tonight," I told her,

huskily, aware of how close her lips were and how easy it would be to slip a hand into the top piece of her dress. I had the rather strong impression she wasn't wearing a bra. The palms of my hands were itching to feel a firm pointed nipple against them.

"I made sure I'd be open for tonight, just in case the new manager was interesting. From what one of the girls told me—she saw you when the owner was taking you around the other day—I figured it was worth my while to be free this evening just in case...though of course, I could call up several of the guys and find at least one free for the night—so I wasn't really putting myself into a position where I'd have to be 'lonely' if I didn't want to." She smiled, her tongue tipped out over the edge of her lips and she moved it back and forth. A very sensual and sexual action to watch.

"Now that we've agreed." I managed, thickly, "to the fact there's a mutual attraction, how long will it take us to develop our relationship into a more fully...relating one?"

When a guy has been around enough he learns to ride with the punches and that was exactly what I was doing! But Gale punches hard and swift—direct blows to the groin!

"You mean, how long will it be before I let you make love to me?" she murmured, lips seeming even closer, moving in a very sexy way over each word as if orgastically devouring them with great pleasure.

"I guess that just about boils it down to the nuts and bolts," I agreed in a very low voice.

"It brings it down to the raw meat of it, Paul. I don't think there is any other way of saying it, without reverting to more blunt terms."

"Probably not."

"Though I'm not against blunt terms, are you?" Her eyebrows arched in question, eyes flashing.

"What ever turns you on, Gale, seems the best way to

say it."

"It turns me on to say a lot of words that polite company frowns at. But a girl has to play it on the man's level to some extent. What turns you on?"

"That dress and what's in it. And the way you talk, low and husky. The perfume you're wearing. Plus the way you come on pretty strong—but honest. I've never met a girl quite like you."

"Frankly, I'm probably the most forward and honestly aggressive girl living here."

"I can believe it."

"If I want something I don't see any reason why I shouldn't go out and make a quick grab for it. Men have always had the right to bluntly ask a girl. Only in the last decades have women realized they should have the same right. Now we claim it. A man takes a girl out for one basic reason, so I've learned: because he wants to screw her."

She said that so casually I didn't even consider the word in any way vulgar—not coming from *her* sexy lips.

"And a girl goes out with a man who she would, at least in time, like to screw. He has the right to try on the first date and if she gives in he thinks what a great thing he walked into! Well, hardly walked…got into is probably closer to the truth. Don't you think? Why shouldn't a girl have that same right? And why should men or women have to play out prolonged games—dinner, dancing, all that jazz, waiting for the drive home when the guy hopes she'll invite him up for a night-cap that might end with breakfast the next morning?

"If a girl is honest about herself she'll realize that when her date turns her on, the only thing she wants is an old-fashioned screw-job. And she'll make it as easy for him as possible. That's why I'm as openly honest with a man as possible. If he doesn't dig this honesty I'm simply not interested in continuing the relationship. I want guys

who come on in a real way and accept me as a human being who has sexual needs that are going to be satisfied one
way or another.

"If they think I'm cheap, that's their problem. I have
the highest respect for myself because I'm honest, not a
phony lying to myself. Sex is here to stay and people are
going to always desire other people. They either play a
waiting game or they honestly admit the truth and dive in
right off."

Well, my own heat was bursting over. I was sweating
by then. My hands felt shaky and my body had that dizzy,
heady feeling that comes when you're all hot and bothered
and about to "dive in" for a real sexual plunge.

"Which is," she continued softly, almost intimately, "a
frank way of saying that I'm not at all against the two of
us getting to be very good and close friends, as soon as
possible."

She was so close now that I almost felt her lips on
mine. It was an illusion quickly broken, because I reached
around her body and our lips automatically merged,
tongues twirling around and around. The taste of her was
delicious. My hard hurt so much that I could hardly stand
it.

I reached up with my left hand and slipped it between
us. She cooperated by moving her torso back slightly. My
hand slid down her neckline, caressing the soft, full, yielding velvet flesh until it was under her dress. My fingers
discovered a pointed nipple, which responded quickly. By
the time I had my palm low enough to cover her tit it was
fully erected and she was pressing up against the squeezing caress.

Her lips suddenly violently sucked on my tongue,
drawing it real deep into her moist mouth.

My hand fondled, gently squeezed her fleshy, supple
breast. It seemed so firm that I was certain it would stand
up at full attention without anything around it but air.

As I had guessed she wasn't wearing a bra. The dress, alone, was designed to fit perfectly around her breasts.

When the kiss broke, she moaned: "Oh, boy, that was great! I almost had an orgasm!"

I made some kind of sound that was supposed to be a chuckle, I guess, and said: "I'm near one myself!"

She reached up to her shoulder and slipped the strap of the dress off its creamy shape, letting the cloth fall low, down to her elbow, then pulled her arm out. The cloth was now far below her right breast. In a moment she'd done the same for the other shoulder-strap. Now Gale was totally exposed from the waist up. What a sight!

And her breasts were completely self-supporting. She told me later that daily exercise kept them in this remarkable shape.

She looked up in a seriously sexy way, arms at her side, and said: "Well, Paul, does that make it simple enough for you?"

I couldn't keep from palming each breast, covering the nipples, which were rosy pink and hard; the areola tightened up about them.

"That feels so good, Paul," she told me in a low-kind of moan, eyes still looking up into mine. "You're real hot, Paul!"

"It sure does feel great," I agreed, fondling and rubbing, squeezing, feeling the texture, the silk, the yielding fullness that was so supple and firm. She had perfectly delightful breasts and I told her as much.

She gave me a slow grin, then said: "I think we should do something about you, too, before we go much further; so that I can have something to do with *my* hands too!"

She leaned close, gently kissing my lips, then opened her mouth wide, sucking on mine until I was able to offer my tongue, which she pulled greedily into her mouth, pressing it up against the roof, wiggling her tongue back and forth. Does she French great! Frenches a man's tool the same way, too!

All this time I was continuing to make the most of her sensually full sexy breasts.

Gale was reaching between my legs, fingers unzipping my pants. Then reaching in, she quickly pulled away everything that could come between her trembling hands and my fully erected hard penis.

Her fingers wrapped around my hard shaft. The other hand cupped my testicles, fondling, then released them, palmed the crown of my penis, rubbing erotic circles. As our kiss broke she squeezed the tip of my manhood, rolling it between her fingers, flicking one over the top.

"You have a nice big prick," she told me throatily. "I'm going to want to do a little deep Frenching, if you don't mind! It feels like it will be good to really French deep. I love Frenching real hard on a man's prick! Kinda like having a real cock…tail. The best drink of all!"

I'll say one thing: her words really charged me!

"You want to finger my cunt?" she offered. "Please, help yourself, honey."

I can't say it was the last thing I would have liked doing.

She stood, releasing me. "Come let it happen the good way, on my big king-size bed!"

She wiggled across the room and I eagerly followed, watching her twitching ass.

Once in front of the bed, she pressed against me, rubbing back and forth against my exposed penis.

"Reach around, unzip the dress," she suggested against my mouth.

This I did, sliding under the gown to find a naked fanny, which I squeezed. She didn't have any panties on, naturally.

"Get the dress off, lover!" she moaned, pleadingly.

This was easy enough. I worked the dress down around her hips and it simply fell away. Then she was actively pulling down my pants and shorts, at the same time stooping until her lips were opposite my naked penis. My pants, by then, made a ring about my legs. While helping me get my feet free, she planted a kiss on the middle of my penis, tongued her way to its crown and flicked up and down on its tip. When my pants and shorts were completely off, she reached up, cupped my testicles, lowered the point of my penis and said: "I'm going to French your cock real deep for a little while. Then we'll get on the bed and have some real fucking fun!"

Her lips surrounded the crown of my penis and I felt the circling movement of her moist tongue making a total exploration. Then she took in more of me until the end of my penis was far back against the roof of her mouth, tongue working in voluptuous jerking motions on the bottom of my throbbing shaft. Her lips pulled on me and it was delightful the way she made little throaty sounds of erotic contentment.

It was hard as hell to keep from losing control, but I wasn't about to ruin a good thing. I simply stood there and enjoyed the pleasure of her mouth and tongue. She moved her lips back and forth, sliding along the length of my penis like an enveloping soft, moist vice, while her tongue kept up its active back and forth movements. It was obvious she really delighted in doing this, that it was something she highly enjoyed. I think she could do this all day without stop; if the man could take that much pleasure without going off like a big gun.

I don't want to sidetrack from a beautiful sexual moment, but it seems a good time to point out several things concerning what Gale was doing—next to how other women many times act—and something in general about the difference between this mod generation of women vs. generations past.

I'm not one to believe in the idea of a sexual revolution having freed women—giving them a chance to do things they never did before.

Sex has been with us for a long time. Naturally. A casual look at ancient sex manuals—classics of erotic literature, they are, too—and one can't escape the fact that there isn't anything under the sun that hasn't been done before, in spades!

What I'm trying to say is that rather than being in a sexual revolution in the manner most people seem to think, I would suggest it is just as possible that the only thing that has been happening in the last decade or so is that people are merely getting to the point where they openly admit to doing things that have always been going on in the bedrooms world wide.

Maybe that's not the right way to put it.

I'd like to consider this from another angle, if I may. First, in our father's and grand-father's time it wasn't considered nice to even talk about sex in public—meaning in the presence of ladies.

What a husband and wife might do or talk about in private is anybody's guess. I wasn't there. I can't make any comments on that. But I don't think it is something new for women to discover the erotic excitement in using what has been considered socially vulgar words concerning the sexual act and all things surrounding it.

Those words have been with us for some time, too. And I find it difficult to imagine that women have only learned their meaning in the last generation. If anything, women in the past generations probably used them just as naturally as a girl like Gale; maybe even more so—who knows?

Nonetheless we've gone through many years of suppression concerning sex. People of America are finally coming around to realizing that sex is a very basic part of life that shouldn't be lied about or hidden under the sheets as if it didn't exist. In fact it is probably the most purely basic element of life—along with eating (and some people enjoy sex more than eating, I might add, without any tongue in cheek, either!)

What is happening today is that adults are simply saying, "To hell with all this crap about acting like we don't know the score!"

They are openly admitting they like sex, are glad it is around and aren't about to play coy little games about the whole thing.

Yet—and here is the big problem: We are all products of a culture that has created a fantastic BASIC LIE about sex. They have openly *denied* their true feelings about sex. But we are faced with a very human and necessary desire to break away from our sexual chains and seek freedom.

In other words while we are mouthing great feelings about sexual freedom, saying how un-hung we are, I believe we're possibly more hung up than many of our parents and grand-parents were.

At one time prostitution was considered a necessary evil; a part of the culture. It was finally smashed, insofar as public willingness to accept it in a more open fashion. Thus it went underground. I've known a few prostitutes. They aren't hard to find. Any major hotel will serve up a helping of women willing to sell their sexual services to interested buyers. And, the interesting thing is, they will give a guy any kind of party he might like—the kind many "respectable" women wouldn't think of offering. Because they have un-hung themselves insofar as having experienced most sexual perversions. They have gone all the way around, 180 degrees, to offer total sexual freedom. Some people who are still out-dated prudes believe that a woman who will openly offer the same kind of activities free-of-charge is probably even more of a whore than the professional prostitute.

Which gets us back to Gale.

While I have tried to reconstruct the conversation which led us to her bedroom and to the point where she anxiously and orgastically went down on me with open visible delight, it has, naturally, been impossible to be totally true to the actual events, insofar as I am only able to remember the important things, able to retell them as a very human memory can—with faults—and have left out much of the unimportant details. She hardly jumped out of her dress for me the minute I stepped into the apartment, though it seemed almost as if she had. And from my retelling I realize I've naturally made it appear this is exactly what she *did* do.

Let me explain it this way.

Here we were, two healthy, mature adult people, both experienced in life and honest with ourselves about the basic physical-sexual needs of our bodies. From the first moment I saw her standing outside her apartment it was obvious as hell this was a girl on the make. Her invitation for a drink wasn't in any way an innocent offer of nothing more than social conversation and booze. She wanted to become friends; her idea of close friendship was a total relating of minds and bodies. Sex, in other words.

In the first place: she probably wouldn't have introduced herself if I hadn't been attractive to her. I wouldn't have accepted her offer if the same didn't apply about my feelings towards her.

Gale made it quickly obvious that we weren't supposed to be merely holding hands and that she wished to develop an immediate sexual thing between us.

Sex at first sight?

I've heard it called that.

Plus this apartment house was as swinging place for singles!

I've also heard guys say they wouldn't go out with a girl who didn't screw on the first date—or at least give every indication they were going to follow through first time or second time out if things developed naturally. Everybody has heard about the "fast" girl who wouldn't go out with a man who didn't make a forward pass on the first date.

Gale didn't consider herself fast. She considered herself adult, lonely, single and hungry for male companionship in a total way. She liked sex in a big way.

She was experienced as hell! Her kisses, her actions and her words left nothing to the imagination.

Yet I believe she was just about as hung-up as the next girl—maybe even more so. She was a product of our society, but she was trying hard to break-free and doing one hell of a job of it.

There is something about a woman that comes on strong like this. Every man likes, at one time or another, to be totally overwhelmed by an aggressively sexy woman. It can be a delightful experience. Sure, many guys like to dominate, because they think it is a threat to their manhood to be the submissive one.

Bullshit! A real man takes things as they are offered and makes the most of it, unafraid of having his male-ego under attack.

With an attractive, aggressive woman like Gale coming on strong like she was, a man is a damned fool not to take all the joys offered. Her attitude was that of an experienced woman who wants the man to know immediately that there isn't a thing in the world she is afraid of doing sexually with a male partner.

When she folded her lips around my erected shaft, moved them up and down, sliding along my penis with that moist, silken embrace, running her tongue back and forth against the sensitive nerves, she was saying more powerfully than any words could have that she worshipped with every nerve a man's penis.

Now, there's a woman!

I don't mind admitting to enjoying a little female worshipping.

Gale could pull and tug on your penis like it was an

all-day sucker. Her tongue just kept wiggling back and forth as those lips kept moving voluptuously on my flesh. She kept sliding her oral embrace up and down. When deeply penetrated beyond her lips, she pressed up with her tongue. She slowly pulled her lips back along my shaft until only the crown was pressed between them, then worked her tongue in flick-like motions up and down against the tip. It was as if she got more pleasure out of it than the man.

I don't know how long this lasted. Long enough to drive me almost beyond control. She seemed to sense when to stop.

Suddenly she released me.

Looking up into my eyes, she said: "Oh, boy, that is so much fun!"

She reached between my legs and squeezed my testicles very sensually. "Now, let's do something more...."

She stood and came into my arms, wiggling her sexual-lips and thighs against my shaft. Her breasts cushioned on my chest, she tongued my lips, then said: "I can't wait for that to stick in!"

We lowered onto the bed but it was going to be some time before we did as she suggested.

Instead I found myself smothered against her breasts— then she was saying: "Oh, go down on me! Please, honey, suck me off good!"

At her urging, we rolled until she was on top of me, then she turned so that her hips were over my face, knees on either side of my head. She was leaning over my lips and hardly had I touched her with a highly erotic tongue kiss than she was enveloping my shaft again between her lips.

This time we didn't stop until both of us had totally exhausted one another.

Well, bluntly put, her pussy just came again and again and when I lost control her mouth just sucked me up then her tongue licked me like wild, like she couldn't get enough of what had spurted out into her mouth. She was just moaning and nearly sobbing in pleasure.

Afterwards, Gale lay alongside me, saying how wonderful it was and how she could hardly wait until I was up and hard enough to do it right with her.

"I want it in me," she murmured softly into my ear. "All the way in me, lover."

She kept her fingers between my legs and kept caressing and squeezing lightly as we talked about sex and things.

You know how it can be with new lovers. They start to talk about how great they think the other is and what kind of things each likes to do. A kind of exploration.

"You know, I just can't get enough to deep Frenching a man like that," she told me. "Oh, but on the other hand, there isn't a thing I don't mind doing with a man. Not a thing in the world!"

I guess you'll want to interview her—and she's one of the most willing, believe me!—so there's no sense of relating some of the things she told me about her early sexual life. Quite interesting.

In any case it wasn't long before she had me hard as a rock. Once I was up big enough she sighed and announced: "My pussy will just devour that big gun of yours!"

Again she took the dominant role. Rolling on top of me she started rubbing her vagina-lips along my shaft. They were really moist, I'll tell you.

She positioned herself so that those well formed breasts, which I'd hardly touched up until now, were close enough so I could easily kiss them.

Her invitation was blunt enough: "Oh, suck my tits, it'll make things more exciting!"

As I pulled one large, rigid nipple into my mouth she moaned and started rubbing harder against my shaft.

I was holding each breast with one hand, moving them outward toward my lips. I moved to the other nipple, then back to the first, keeping almost a perfect rhythm with her hip actions.

Suddenly she lost control and moved her hips so that the point of my shaft was almost at the entrance to her vagina, which she circled around until it had captured me. She surged down and I found myself engulfed between the moist, slippery vice of her lover-lips. She moved up and down in slow, grinding movements that plunged me deeply within her and then circled me almost all the way out.

She kept moaning and sobbing with delight, all the time looking excitedly into my eyes. I started fondling her breasts with my hands and she gulped hard in pleasure. It was obvious that she liked that kind of action, so I continued squeezing her fleshy breasts, aware of the erected points of her nipples.

All at once she went crazy, fairly slamming down against me, rising up and slamming down, writhing wildly with every thrusting surge of our bodies which were both in perfect union.

I met each plunge of her hips with an upward thrust until both of us were sweating and to the edge of orgasm. I'm sure we achieved climax almost together. It was a beautiful experience, I'll tell you!

After that both of us were exhausted beyond our ability to even speak. We fell asleep in each other's arms. Much later I had all the chance I needed to feast on her lovely breasts.

We made love a couple of times during the night and I didn't leave her apartment until the next morning, after a delicious breakfast of eggs and bacon—and a good-bye sexual union that made me almost limp back to my own place, where I showered and then fell exhaustedly on the bed to sleep until well-past noon.

That was my first experience with Gale, though hardly my last. She's very popular, but always finds time for "the manager"—especially around rent time. She always pays the rent, though it is late once in a while and I believe she makes sure I'm kept happy if for no other reason but to be sure I don't put on the screws about late payments.

We've never been together socially except in bed, unless it is at a party, which is something totally different. There are quite a few that go on at the apartment. One person or another is giving a party, almost every week-end. Usually anybody can drop in. Most of the time it is a bring-your-own-bottle affair, so if for no other reason, you're more than welcomed. Few people can drink a whole fifth all by themselves, naturally. But, as Gale says, "they have limp dicks!"

As for the parties, well, they can be anything from normal, casual drinking cocktail affairs to a few blowout sexual orgies.

I've enjoyed every party given. Almost always there is some willing girl to either have a great time with in a bedroom, the one there or your's. It is easy enough to just casually suggest going down to your place for a little more private conversation. Almost always the girl will be willing. Perhaps that's because you don't make the mistake of asking a girl who hasn't offered the right signals. And they aren't as brazen as the ones that Gale might give. Every guy knows the signals and he'd be a damned fool not to grab what can be had.

There are very little shy games, no childish flirtations just for the kick of it. If somebody flirts and there's a follow-through, you can bet there's a damned good chance of something interestingly intimate in the offer.

It isn't that every girl is willing to spread goodies to every man—or that I'm the most exciting male in the world—but simply that there are enough women there who are willing to swing with a guy who knows the ropes.

The groovy swingers immediately get to know one another.

Example: It wasn't long before Gale was going out of her way to introduce me to certain girls who lived at the apartment. A short conversation with said girl indicated that she was interested in a mature relationship. Gale had made the introduction because she considered me a groovy bedroom partner and wanted to make sure the swingers at the apartment who might be interested in exploring bedroom games with me were given their chance. In other words: she saw to it that I almost immediately learned who was really in-the-groove and let the girls know me.

There are very few jealousies. Very few serious coupling off. When things get serious between a girl and guy it isn't long before they just stop being part of the party-group. Some end up getting married and moving away. For the most part the statement "for singles only" means just that: unattached unmarried looking for total companionship. Most don't want serious involvements.

That's why the place is great for singles. And even if it isn't screwing every day and night—unless that's what you want, and are lucky enough to get that kind of service all the time—any guy and gal will get the full share of sexual adventures. In blunt terms: it's a heaven for people who want to swing all the way, no questions asked.

* * * * * * *

While Paul had gone into some detail about the parties, I edited this portion out since others had told me quite a bit about them in a lot of detail. I have kept Paul's story down to the bare facts of importance concerning his own personal introduction to the apartment and his observations concerning it and the people who live there.

Not everybody was as totally involved in the party and swinging sexual activities as Paul or Gale. But before recording some of the various attitudes I came across at the apartment "for singles only", it might be proper to put down my rather interesting interview with Gale, the girl who had introduced Paul to the swingers. She wasn't the first interviewed, nor the last, though the only one with whom I became involved in a sexual way. It was impossible to ignore her blatant offers. She's without question down right basic and bluntly seductive!

As Paul pointed out, Gale had her hang-ups; but regardless, she was a very aggressive and dominating young woman who could easily overwhelm almost any male animal.

I didn't expect what I found, even with the warning Paul had offered before the interview and in his own material concerning Gale. One never expects what he hears from others to be actual truth.

But more important was the insights her interview gave. We have seen Gale from Paul's point-of-view. Now a slightly different picture forms when she tells her own story.

CHAPTER TWO

GALE

Her first statement, once I'd set up the tape-recorder and she had served both of us with excellent martinis, was: "Are you going to seduce me tonight?"

I looked at Gale, aware of the kind of woman she was from several sources. I remembered what Paul had told me about her; and it was difficult to keep from finding her highly exciting. I could hardly add anything to what my friend already said concerning her attractiveness and sensuality.

She was dressed in slacks, a little under-size to reveal a bit more than it should around the crotch, and a V-necked, tight sweater. The way her breasts had moved when she walked indicated that this woman wasn't wearing a bra.

"I didn't come here for that reason," I pointed out as professionally as possible. But I'll honestly admit that the idea was far from unappealing.

"I read some of your books, Mr. Davis and—"

"Might as well call me Carson," I offered.

"That's friendly enough," she agreed with a pleased smile. "But, anyway, Carson, I was saying I that I read some of your books and they are pretty far-out."

"In what way?" I found her statement intriguing considering what I already knew about this woman.

"Well, that people actually talk like that."

"You don't believe in talking like that?"

She laughed brightly, then said: "No, didn't mean it quite like...well, you see I really get a big bang talking about sex in the raw. But I didn't know other people were like me."

"Most of us aren't that different," I pointed out. "There are all kinds of people in the world. Nobody is exactly original, nor are they exactly carbon-copies of others. There are simply all shades of human beings. If you are a certain way you can expect there must be many hundreds of thousands, millions much like you to some extent. Even if with a difference. We bring to our particular type all the elements of our experience which finally, in the end, defines our personal style."

"That's an interesting idea," she told me in a thoughtful voice. "Maybe you're right. One always thinks of themselves as being totally different from everybody else. Are we all the same under our outer shells?"

"Probably not exactly—but enough so that an alien from outer space might say, I can't tell them apart, they all look, sound and think alike!"

We both laughed at that, then she asked: "Then maybe there's really nothing wrong with my talking...well what some people call dirty and vulgar about the sexual act."

"Do you think there is something wrong?"

"Well, society always has frowned on such words as prick and fuck and screw and cunt. People are sure to be shocked if you come right out and use such words in so-called polite company."

"What is your feeling about it?"

"What?"

"The use of sexual words such as you mentioned?"

"I use them, don't I?"

"But in public?"

"No. Hardly." Her face blushed at this point and as she realized this she said: "But what a kick to use them! When I can. See, I do get embarrassed, simply thinking of doing such a thing. I mean in public and all that. Maybe they're just so...personally intimate, a real turn on to me."

"When do you use such words?"

"Not enough to satisfy my hairy damned tastes," she announced. "But they sure get me kinda worked up, all over. I kind of get a thrill—almost like a small little cum—when I say something like fuck or I want your cock in my screaming wet pussy. If a guy says fuck while we're fucking, I just cream all over his back big prick. If he keeps saying that to me, I just keep doing wild all over. It makes me cum like wild."

She shivered visibly from the statement. "See what I mean? Oh, this is going to be fun, because I just know I can say anything I want to you and you aren't going to be shocked or something like that. And if I cum, well, you won't mind too much, I'd imagine! Right? How delicious. I'm almost dong it right now!"

She literally squirmed. "You don't mind? Me talking this way?"

"Just tell me about yourself in any manner you wish."

"That's great. Just anything I want to say, in any way I desire. But what?"

"Well, you might start with the apartment."

"Do I have to start there? From reading some of your books the people talk about their early sexual experiences. Don't you want to hear something about them? About how my...well, what...my first cock did to me?"

"Do you think this might have any purpose in revealing your attitudes and feelings of the present?"

"I don't know." She sounded honestly puzzled, so I decided to fire her some questions. "But I want to let you know all about me."

"Well, tell me, when did you start feeling the urge to

become a swinging bachelor-girl?"

"I don't know if I ever *didn't* feel the urge. Don't you think most people want to swing, but don't have the guts to do it? One guy said to me: 'All that pussy!' and I just laughed and told him: 'All that cock…fucking good cock.' But most guys…well they're all uptight about sex. About swinging. They claim no way, but they all want to have it at least once."

"Probably there are a lot of people like that and—"

She laughed, cutting into my words. "Of course they all want sex, even the screwed-up prudes who don't know anything about sex because they are afraid of it. I've known a few in my life. In fact, my sister was a real prude. She's never gotten married. Hasn't had a man, either. But she fingers herself. I know *that* much, because I happened to step into the bathroom one afternoon to find her sitting on the john, legs spread wide, naked, her fingers making double-time action. I was surprised, you can bet your sweet hard cock on that—but she was horrified.

"We never talked about it. I left immediately and had a good laugh. She's a couple of years older than me. We used to talk about boys and sex, though, before and afterwards. We simply never mentioned what I'd seen her doing. Of course, I did the same thing but was smart enough to lock the bathroom door so nobody could catch me fingering my pussy like wild. I guess she got to locking the door, too, after that!

"She was always interested in my sexual adventures. Used to question me endlessly. In a subtle way. But what she wanted was all the gory details. I didn't tell her the real truth—at least not most of the time. First I simply told her lies. Saying I'd done things with boys I'd never done. Like saying I'd gone down on my date. She thought that was horrid. But I'll bet the next time she was in the bathroom she was thinking about how it might be to be sucking cock! But she's too hung-up to have sexual relations with a guy. She'd be better off if she became a Lesbian, don't you think?"

"How's that?" I inquired carefully.

"Well, at least she'd be relating to *some* one! As it is she just goes into her room and rubs her meat, all alone and feeling guilty."

"What has she got against men?"

"Nothing. Nothing at all. And never puts anything against them, you can bet on that!" Gale laughed and then said more seriously: "She thinks sex is dirty. She's afraid of getting pregnant. She's afraid of sex and men and—oh, hell, is she all screwed up!"

"What caused her to be that way?"

"How do I know? Maybe because it is the way the folks raised us. They would say things like 'don't touch yourself down there,' as if it were some dirty place filled with creepy germs. If it is I've had some real germ warfare with a lot of cocks!"

"Your folks taught you that sex was dirty?"

"Well, not in so many words. Simply that a girl should wait until she is married."

"Did you?"

"Hell no! What do you think I am? Square? Hell. I had my first cock when I was seventeen in the back seat of his car. I couldn't keep my hands off him. We started to neck and I just had to feel his cock. I desperately wanted to feel what a man had between his legs. I'd known just about what to expect from stories other girls told. I was surprised how big and hard a man's prick can be. I wondered how it could get in me! So big! I was almost afraid it would hurt me terribly. But my pussy was so wet and hot...well, nature takes its natural course. Of course!"

"I take it that you had considered giving yourself to this guy for some time?"

"Hardly this one. But I had considered doing it with *some*one! I figured I was old enough. I'm *not* like my sister. She is really sick. I don't think she'll ever get married. I just don't understand such people. They make me ill even thinking about it. Real angry! Believe me."

"You don't consider them simply moral people living by their own standards?"

"Hell no! They aren't any more moral than I am and...."

"I don't think they are, either. But they can be just as moral, if they are living by their own personal code of ethics. And just as immoral as a human being can be by not living by the ethical code that will give them the most happiness."

She spat out, almost furiously: "All they want to do is get screwed sexually without getting involved with the sexual act. They stay in rooms beating their meat, thinking about all things they would like to do, but afraid to do them. They get screwed silly in their perverted sick little minds! Why don't they come on out and join the world!"

"And what would that involve?"

"Rubbing their hot little groins against somebody— even members of their own sex! Rather than having it by themselves. Join the world and start rubbing groins!" She laughed and added: "That's quite a way of putting it. Groin rubbing. I really *love* rubbing my groin against a man's. I especially like going down on a guy. I've always been terrible oral. Lips are sensitive."

She was thoughtful for a moment, then said: "You know, it was some time before I learned the real meaning of living. Well, about life. Want me to tell you about it?"

"Talk about anything that comes into your mind, Gale," I offered grandly, figuring this would be one portion that I could edit out later. In most taped interviews it is necessary to cut out a lot of pointless statements made by the subject; it is also necessary to let them talk about anything they wish to, in order for the important material to come out. At times it is quite a job sifting the good from the bad, even necessary to make bridges in order to have a smoothly running case history. I expected this to be one of those times.

"You see, as I've pointed out, my family was, probably, pretty average in many ways. The folks didn't talk about sex and one could imagine they didn't screw, if it weren't for the fact they had two daughters. I never could imagine my mother and father in bed together. But then I've learned most kids can't imagine such a thing. Though, I'll admit, my dad was pretty good looking. A strong man who liked sports—actively and as a watcher. A man like that likes his sex in the raw.

"He was dominant. He dominated the whole house. The only time you could really get away from the domination was when you were on a date—and even then he was there, silently, invisible, screaming in your mind. Like, we couldn't stay out too late. Time-limit depended on where we were going and who the boy was. The funny thing is that dad always checked out the boys in real detail, both by their looks and what they said. He had to talk to them before he would let me leave for a date. He gave them the subtle third-degree—he had studied to be a lawyer in college, though never made the final exams. We never knew what the deadline was until after dad had finished his little game, at which time he'd say what time we should be back home.

"The funny part about it was the guys he felt were 'dangerous' turned out to be the harmless ones. Maybe because of the time-limit, though I doubt that. For the ones he felt were safe he would give me a later deadline for returning home—and it was with these I had my best swinging times. Heck, to be honest, with many of them...well, we'd fuck our brains out."

"You make it sound like you were fairly experienced very young."

"Not really. But I had my kicks. There's quite a difference between teen-age making-out, as we called it, and adult swinging. Making-out meant, to me, up to the age of seventeen, nothing more than deep tongue kissing and sometimes a few petting-games—though it was some time before such games turned into pussy petting, if you know what I mean!"

"Why don't you tell me exactly what you mean?"

"Details?"

"Whatever you think necessary."

She grinned seductively and then leaned close to me, as if confiding. "Well, at first it was free breast-feeling. The first time a guy put his hand on my breasts I almost fainted. Oh, did it feel great. I'd squeezed and fondled my own breasts when in bed. You know, running my hands up under my nightie and palming them. Working my tits until they got very hard. I kept wanting to suck and lick them. You know how it is. Well maybe you don't. I mean about breasts. Since you don't have them. Not like a girl, anyway, of course.

"But I've known guys who admitted to wishing they could get their cocks in their mouths. Not that they were homosexual or anything like that. Just that they thought the idea of lips around their large hard meat would feel great. The first guy to admit that to me did so after I'd done some real lip-service to his prick. He said how great it was. Then we got to talking about sex and teen-age experience and things. He just came out and said there had been times when he was a kid, banging his meat, that he wished it was possible to get it in his mouth. Said it was the greatest thing when a girl first did it to him.

"He was fifteen and with his aunt—who was only couple of years older than him. Some of the things they had done. She wouldn't let him stick her pussy—because that would be degenerate. But she liked to go down on a man and did it quite a few times with him.

"Boy, what I've heard about people. I never thought

relatives could really do such things together. It is rather perverted, don't you think?"

"Not particularly the most desirable thing," I admitted. "But certainly not the most perverted thing. Illegal and all that, socially condemned, a Taboo item in all societies. But certainly on the low end of degenerate type acts. Still, never mind that. We aren't in the business of making judgments. Just continue."

She laughed and leaned even closer until I could smell the scent of her perfume. "I know just what you mean. Like a girl bending all the way over, wiggling her little ass at a guy who has a blasted paddle in his hand, which he slaps hard against her butt. That's perverted. I've known guys who wanted to do that to me—but I'm not in that kind of bag! Never! I guess there are some other things, too. A girl I knew admitted to taking a hotdog and sticking it up her pussy. Said it was almost like a man's cock—not as hard, but meaty. She'd screw herself silly with it time and again. Claimed she could get all kinds of cums by working the end back and forth in her pussy. That's perverted, too! Or fingering your own...back door.

"I never dreamed people would do things like that to themselves. I've had guys do it to me—but that's something different. It can be just part of the sex-play. Especially when they are fingering your pussy at the same time—or sticking their cock in you. That's something when a guy fingers your back door while screwing your pussy off! But its all part of a sex-play. Like squeezing your breasts while pumping your cunt."

She was leaning very close and I could get a good view of her neckline. A very sexually exciting sight.

She noticed the direction of my gaze and grinned. Leaning back, a knowing, pleased expression on her face, she asked: "Do you find me sexy?"

"You're a very attractive woman."

"Bet Paul—and some of the guys—told you all about

me, didn't they?"

"Well, a lot has been said and—"

"Oh, come on. Tell me what they said. I'd be delighted. Did they say I was a good lay? That I liked to screw a man's cock right off? That I fucked great?" Her eyes flashed with pleasure. "I sure to hell would like to know what guys say about me behind my back. I know girls talk something wild. Did you know that?"

"It's quite common. Most men don't realize that."

"That's funny, isn't it? Girls really talk about their lovers."

She was quiet for a moment, then said:

"Well, I got a little off the point, didn't I? I was telling you about my father and how he screened guys. The one who first fucked me was high on his list of clean-cut types. Safe, in other words. Dad would have probably killed me if he'd known I was pussy-sucking a man's cock—well, he was only a young man, but he screwed pretty good.

"Though I was telling you about the first experiences. When a guy first touched my breasts I almost passed out with the pleasure it gave. But I refused to let him take off my sweater or bra. Though it wasn't long—maybe a couple of months—before I'd let a steady date get some real good feels. I remember the first time. I was just as anxious as the guy. He couldn't wait. He pulled my sweater up over my bra—like this."

Gale pulled her sweater up until her breasts were totally exposed under it. "See, like this.

"Then he undid my bra and just worked one breast loose so he could fondle and suck tittie. Oh, it was so good. And terribly painful—meaning that it is really hard on a girl when she gets all excited but won't go all the way. I wasn't about to go all the way.

"By the time I was seventeen, with cherry still intact, I'd done just about everything short of screwing. But oh how I wanted one in me. I'd even jerked a boy off. It was fun seeing all that juice explode from his cock. I still like to watch a guy go off—especially when he's brimming full of...lover's wine! Love eating him, too. What a juicy cocktail a big prick can give a girl. A real tail of the cock! Oh, that reminds me!"

I had almost choked on the sight of her naked breasts. The nipples were taunt and tempting.

She covered herself and then smiling as if at some secret, Gale said: "There was this one guy who really dug having me do—well, to be truthful it was my first husband. Now why didn't I come out and say that right from the beginning? Oh, well. The thing is that my first husband dug having me jerk him off and I'd do it a lot of times. We'd take showers together and I'd reach between his legs and jerk away until he discharged. Sometimes I was in the way. I'd do it over the john with him, too. It was a good thing to do if I wanted to enjoy giving him a good blow job, because he could go off pretty easily. We had quite a time during the first months of our marriage. I mean, sexually. He would go off too soon."

"That's fairly normal with a guy who isn't too experienced sexually," I commented.

"Well, he hadn't been too experienced when I met him. But we enjoyed doing a lot of things—I mean, no hang-ups about exploration. We simply learned it was best if I jerked him off first. It kind of simmered him down a bit. Then I could do my lip work on his limp meat until it got good and juicy hard. Since I like doing that to a man, the longer it lasts the more fun. A guy can finger me or even give me some deep cunt Frenching. A good-old-fashioned sixty-nine is just about the best—outside of screwing the regular way. And that can be in any position, as far as I'm concerned.

"Some girls don't dig dog-fashion screwing. I like it. Kind of different. They say it isn't supposed to give a girl as much pleasure, physically, as other positions, because a man's cock isn't really hitting her in the right way. But, believe me it is thrilling. Maybe because...well, there's something orgasmic about it! A guy can sometimes reach under you and squeeze your breasts, or even finger the lips of your pussy, kind of...real fun, if you know what I mean."

I nodded, realizing that one reason a woman would like this kind of position was because she considered sex dirty and found herself orgasmic stimulated when entering into an act that was considered animal. The theory being that if you're going to fall in the gutter you might as well enjoy getting really messed up.

"Psychologically the woman gets a thrill out of such a position because she considers it even more perverted than more conventional positions. This is the same reason for people liking anal intercourse or involving themselves in sadistic sex. If you are beaten enough, to the point where it is impossible to refuse doing anything asked, then you are relieved of any guilt-feelings, simply because it has been taken out of your hands—thus it isn't your fault being forced into a sexual act that gives pleasure you consciously believe is perverted and dirty. And the funny thing that the so-called spankings are controlled and don't really hurt at all. But silly."

I couldn't help wondering if Gale was as un-hung sexually as she claimed.

"Well," she continued after a moment of silence, "My first husband wasn't the best in bed, that was for sure. But he was willing to try and got better. Though while he was getting better, I was getting more and more anxious. I kept wondering what it would be like with other guys. Better lovers. I was turned-on!"

"How much?"

"In what way?" she countered, obviously puzzled by the exact meaning of my question.

"Well, just how turned on were you? In other words,

did you cheat?"

"Hell, no! I don't believe in cheating. After all, a marriage is a contract—forgetting the legal bit. I do believe that when people get married they should keep totally loyal to one another. What's the point, otherwise? You might as well be merely living with somebody, with the understanding that it's free sex all the way, but there's nothing wrong with a few outside relationships. Though I don't even believe in that! Sure, there's the argument one gets companionship and everybody needs that thing! One way or another. But as far as I'm concerned, when two people have an arrangement, living together, it is ethical and moral that they remain loyal to one another—at least as far as their verbal agreement is concerned.

"Well, what I'm trying to say is that there are couples living together—hell, even married couples—who think nothing of swapping partners. I don't dig that scene. I really don't think it makes much sense. At least, not for me!

"If a person wants to have more than one lover they should live by themselves. It is different if you are on a date with some guy and things are arranged where you get together with another couple to have a real sexy orgy. That's the whole scene. The point is you both might be screwing each other silly. But just for kicks you decide to get together with another couple who digs a real wild sex party with more than one partner involved in sexual action—and there's nothing wrong with that, just so long as everybody is a mature adult. Don't you agree?"

I said: "Very important to be consenting adults, not doing anything to harm anybody. Yes. That's important."

"Like, dig this. I was dating a guy and we were pretty loose about sex. Meaning we both dug just about everything and never made any bones about it. We liked to screw each other in every possible way. We talked sex. We talked about all the possible ways a person could do it and got to talking about how it is possible for more than two people to be active in sexual relations.

"You see, I'd already had some experience in this kind of thing. Like, a case in point, once I was with two brothers. I'd dated one for some time—and we'd fucked like wild. I met the other. He asked me out. Guess his brother told him how great a lay I was. We hit it off right on the first date. This, by the way, happened after my first marriage was on the rocks. Like finished, you understand.

"Well, the second brother had one hell of a big cock. A real long beautiful, lovely arching prick. Oh, how great it felt going in and out of my pussy. He'd get me real ready and moist with his tongue and lips—like doing me up real pink with deep cunt-kisses. Then when he inserted his big long cock into me—oh, it was like some kind of flag-pole. He was wonderful.

"And, sure, being a woman I realize it isn't how long they make it, but how they make it long—meaning, naturally, nice and long-lasting! A small prick is just as wonderful as a big one, insofar as tickling a girl's pussy to orgasm. But he was great and not only long in cock-length, but long is screwing-time. He gave me slow, lingering deeply penetrating, right to the thick base of his shaft, and then pull out so slow I could have a couple of cums just like that.

"Well, we talked about the fact I was dating both of them. Meaning, both brothers. How I'd screwed with each brother. No bones made about that! You understand. And he asked me, like a stupid ass, which brother was best. Like, he wanted to know he was better than his brother. And I said both of them were damned good and I'd have nothing against fucking both at once.

"He thought that idea was great. Like, he jumped all over himself saying it would really be something. Then he started suggesting all the things we could do as a threesome. As it turned out, he and his brother had done it with a girl together. A whore, in Mexico, he said. He told me what the prostitute did. Like sucking and fucking at one time. The whole idea sounded just simply great. In fact, so damned fantastic I almost experienced a cum thinking about it.

"So they very next day—Saturday, if I remember right—I went over to his brother's pad and we screwed silly. I went down on both of them at once. Well, like they were stripped and I was stripped and I just looked at those two ding-dong pricks hanging between their legs and I damned well wished to hell I could have both in my mouth at once. So I fell to my knees before them and taking my ever-loving time went from one limp prick to the other. I mouthed the end of one brother, then mouthed the crown of the other. Each time I returned to a brother's cock it was bigger. I started really getting a mouthful of each, just sliding my lips down until the tip was between my lips. Then I tongued the blasting crown and tip like wild. Released the hardening cock and went to the other brother to give him a little mouth-thrill. It was really something, I'll tell you. Each was a little different in shape and size and I found it far more thrilling than simply working on one guy alone.

"I kept it up until my pussy was so hot I couldn't stand it. And they were up like two poles. While mouthing on one brother's gun, I fondled and squeezed the other's.

"Well, I just had to have something in my hot moist cunt and made my wishes very clear.

"So we went to town. Right in the living room. On the floor. I couldn't wait. I simply lay down on my back on the wall-to-wall carpet, opened my mouth wide, spread my thighs and a few moments later captured myself two wonderful male guns.

"You know, I've often thought about this kind of thing. Like, oh, it would be simply wonderful to have a dozen, maybe twenty or thirty beautiful man-cocks all in a line. I'd go down the line feasting on each one for a moment. Then moving on to the other male-cock and filling my mouth with that orgastically beautiful thing.

"You can't imagine how beautiful a man's big fat cock is to me. And the lovely soft, mushy balls that get so firm and tensed up after a little loving."

Without warning, Gale just reached out and placed a hand between my legs. "Is yours big?"

The sensation that ripped up through my whole body at this sudden and unexpected attack made me dizzy.

Her fingers explored and squeezed and I was beginning to respond very quickly.

Then just as suddenly she withdrew her hand, saying: "You have some real big meat. I sure hope you give me a meal on it before the evening is up."

I was slightly stunned.

She apparently realized my surprise and said, in a slightly husky, laughing voice: "I couldn't help myself. Talking about hard cocks I couldn't help wondering how big yours was. And you can bet your hard cock that I'll go down on it before the night is over. I simply can't wait. Well, no. That's not quite true. The waiting makes it even more exciting. Kind of torturing myself. Teasing my pussy.

"Well, anyway. I was saying that I didn't think married people should cheat. If they want something other than their spouse they should call it a day. Finish the marriage. Same for people living together.

"That's why this kind of apartment is simply great! I can get all the companionship I wish. So I don't have to live with some stud artist. I can get myself a good wild screw-job just about any time of day and night. Every guy here knows I have a hot pussy that needs a hard cock to service it one hell of a lot. Like, they know I'm sexy and need a man and they accept me as something great. This place is like a wonderful meat market for me. Sausages all over the play.

"Not all the girls are as willing to give it out as often as I do. The guys think I'm a good thing. Maybe they have some idea I'm a kind of tramp. But I don't think of myself in that way. I consider myself simply an honest woman. I dig sex. I just love cocks. I mean...really love them! I want them all the time. Even while working I think about how lovely it would be to be sitting on a man's hard shaft.

Like working and having a man's cock inserted in my pussy.

"Well, put it this way. There are some Lesbian's I've known who have dildos. You know what they are, I guess. And one told me how great it was to sit in front of the television at night totally naked with the dildo stuck in her cunt.

"I wouldn't dig that scene. But I certainly wouldn't mind a real cock inside me, twitching and alive. Just inside me. Nothing happening. Just aware of a man's hard responding to the moist walls of my loving sex hole squeezed around his flesh.

"Know what I mean?"

The way she said it and the silence that immediately accented her statement demanded an answer.

So I said: "You almost sound like you're not only highly sexed, but almost over-sexed." The statement was made in light humor and she didn't take it seriously.

"I'd just love to squeeze your love-gun." She writhed slightly, then placed a hand between her own legs, slowly moving it upwards. "It is so hot. You know that. I'm oh so hot. I have a hot, wet pussy wanting something in it. It hurts a girl, you know."

Then looking between my legs, she said: "It hurts a man, too, doesn't it?"

I was still in full erection from her boldly brazen hand-caress and to be quite truthful hurting like hell!

Nonetheless I managed to remain totally cold-blooded and professional.

"You were telling me about your first marriage."

"Oh, that. A bore, really. He was okay, like I said. But not enough for me. I don't mean I didn't love him. The only thing is that we'd gotten married too young. I was nineteen. The marriage lasted two years. By then I simply couldn't take it any longer. I'd see other guys and realize I really wanted to screw the shit out of them. It got to the point where I couldn't stand it any longer. I would think of some guy at work, or some fellow I'd seen on the street and wondered about him while letting my husband stick me with his cock. It got to the point where I was mentally screwing these other guys while being taken by my husband. That's almost cheating!

"That's when I decided it wasn't any good. When a girl starts doing something like that she isn't in love with her husband. And that's for sure! I mean, sometimes anybody might do that now and then. But when it gets to the point where you're always fucking the other guy, not the one in you, there's something wrong. I called it off. I simply told him one day that I wanted a divorce. He couldn't believe it. I finally ended up telling him the total truth. When he heard that he almost killed me.

"Well, I mean, he started getting violent. He actually raped me that night. Ripped off my clothing and violently yanked my legs apart and rammed himself in. When he was finished he said I could have my 'fucking divorce'— to put it in his words. I guess no man can take the kind of ego-blast I'd given him. I hadn't meant to hurt him. But, like I said, I've learned a lot since I was a teenager.

"After splitting with husband number one I made the scene for real. Like taking up with one cock after another. But I got tired of that, then. I was still young enough to feel guilty about sex. I didn't believe what I was doing was exactly right. And I still wanted love. Plus, there wasn't a place like this.

"To be brutally frank, I got lonely.

"I was working as a typist in an insurance firm. One of the salesmen started dating me. We didn't screw. Then on our fifth or seventh date he asked me to marry him. I really don't know to this day why I accepted. We went to Las Vegas and got married. Right then. The date had been on a Friday, so we had the weekend. I guess I screwed his ass off on our 'honeymoon'. The marriage lasted longer than it should have. For over a year. We simply didn't make it sexually.

"You see, he wouldn't let me go down on him and he wouldn't go down on me. Finger me, but no mouth to sex-mouth Frenching. I went frantic, really. But I tried to make it go. When I learned he was having an affair with another woman...well, that was it! What hurt the most was he would go down on her and let this bitch feast a meal on his cock. Turned out that he felt a wife was one thing and a woman who did things like that was a whore. I never understood how he got the idea that I was all that 'innocent'. Though I did give a lot of thought about the fact that I'd never been able to really come out and tell him the truth about my own feelings. "In any case, when I learned he was cheating, I simply picked myself up a couple of guys at a bar, brought them home and made sure they were still there bed with me when husband number two returned home from work. He walked in on quite a scene.

"I was straddling one guy, with his thick cock in my pussy, wiggling like hell, while the other stood over him, facing me, with his big prick in my mouth and my arms around his hips, hands squeezing his butt.

"I realize it was a dirty and sick thing to do, now. But at the time it seemed logical enough.

"My husband went into a rage, but I laughed and told him I knew about his little girl-friend and that we were finished. Then I left the house with the two guys I'd picked up, went to a motel with them and spent the night having a great orgy. I mean a really wild one. We fucked every hole

I had and then some. I couldn't get enough of them.

"It took me some time to really settle down and accept things as they really are."

"Which is?" I inquired when she was silent for a moment.

"Screwing is fun. You don't have to be married to have yourself a hell of a ball—and cock!" She laughed, then said: "Cock and balls! You know how they say a girl is a piece of tail? Well, I've realized that a guy is a cock-tail!"

Somehow the humor of her statement struck me right. I laughed, until suddenly realizing she had her hands between my legs, my zipper pulled down and fingers exploring under my jocks. I hadn't even realized she was going at me until I felt her fingers against naked flesh.

"My, my, you really have a nice one," she announced throatily.

The way she was caressing and squeezing me made it impossible to keep from responding in a highly charged way. I kept thinking about her naked breasts under the sweater. What she was doing certainly made it impossible to actually call things off at this point.

Before I knew it, Gale was between my legs, her lips covering the crown of my penis. The sensations her mouth and tongue drove through me were far too great to ignore.

As I've pointed out many times before, I'm not at all interested in detailing my own personal sexual experiences. Only when some important point is involved will I relate any information at all. It is enough to say that Gale lived up to what Paul had reported about her.

She drove the two of us beyond the point of no return. We totally consumed our passions and later continued with the interview as if nothing had happened to interrupt it.

"Tell me about your feelings concerning the apartment," was my first suggestion once we'd returned our attention to the subject of the interview.

"What do you want to know?" she inquired, smiling very seductively up at me. She was still naked—and for that matter, so was I.

"In general, first, what type of person, do you believe, picks this kind of place to live?"

Her laugh almost was mocking. "Are you kidding? Naturally everybody is a swinger. Well of sorts. They don't all do it like I do. They all have their own way of swinging. But...if they aren't into free sexual expression...well they don't get an apartment here. Requirement number one: Be a sophisticated swinger who realizes that sex is here to stay and they want to get a good healthy portion of it. Like, want to experience life. They believe we only live once. Dig?"

"Is that all there is to it?"

She pursed her lips in thought, then said:

"Well, I guess everybody who is single, living alone, knows what it is like to be lonely. It can be pretty hard. Before I discovered this place I was getting pretty un-hung emotionally. Either I went out and picked up some guy at a bar—and there are plenty of places around town where singles can go to get picked up—or I stayed home, biting my nails, watching tired television shows and wishing there was something better to do. One can get terribly tired of watching television or reading books, all alone. And when you are between boy friends—it is hard! I never liked picking guys up, too much. It seemed...well, I felt a little cheap. But what is a girl with a healthy body supposed to do? How many times can you get together with the girls or with your family?

"A guy named Mark...no need to know his last name... was responsible for exposing me to this apartment. I met him through a girl friend. He was living here. The first time he invited me over to his pad I didn't know what to expect. It was about three in the afternoon—Saturday, if

I'm right—maybe a holiday—it doesn't matter. In any case what I walked into was wild. There was a swinging pool-side party going on. Everybody was in bikinis—even the men had on those low cut, tight suits that show off the big bulge of their sex-guns. I never saw so many big guns at one place except on the beach. But all these guys look like swinging cats on the make and the girls were just the same. You've seen one of the parties?"

I nodded. (In the next case history such a party is detailed to some extent.)

"Well the girls were falling all over themselves to make themselves attractive and interesting to the guys—same for the men. Mark took me up to his pad. There I was in for a surprise. He had a friend in his bedroom, sticking it to a girl. They were both naked as they had been born.

"I'd let Mark bang it to me and we were both pretty open about sex—so there wasn't any attempt to make excuses. His friend laughed when we walked in. He was on his back with the girl straddling his hips—in full lovely penetration. 'Sorry about interrupting,' was Mark's casual statement. The girl turned, grinned, said: 'Why don't you join us?'

"Well, Mark looked at me with a big question mark on his face. I hesitated, then shrugged. So the girl invited Mark to strip down and give her a mouthful. The two of us stripped and I was told to squat down over the other guy's face so he could have a pussy meal while Mark stood in front of me, facing the girl who worked his cock to full erection with her mouth. I started fingering him from the back, squeezing his testicles while my pussy was given a real working over by this guy lying on the bed. Oh, that was an orgiastic time. Halfway through Mark turned so I could go down on him. At that point the other girl really started grinding away at her boy friend's stick. I guess we almost came at once.

"Afterwards we talked, smoked and drank. The guy's name was Jim—the girl, I think, Carol. Before long Jim asked if I wanted to go into the bedroom with him. I looked at Mark who nodded it was all right with him. Carol moaned, saying: 'Can't we all do it together some more?'

"It was agreed, so we all went into the bedroom. This time I lay on my back while Jim let me go down on him and Mark went down on me, while Carol managed to keep his cock happy with hands and finally mouth. Like, Mark was positioned between my legs, and his rear sticking up. Carol simply played with him, using her fingers until he had a big hard. Apparently Mark couldn't take it any more than she could, because he pulled away from me and the two of them lay on the bed next to Jim and me. Jim turned around so we were in a sixty-nine position and we continued for some time. Later I got on top of him and Mark mounted my fanny, entering doggie fashion while Jim grabbed Carol so he could go down on her.

"Later another couple joined us and the girl liked both men and women that way. Carol got on her back, this new girl straddled her face while going down on Jim. The new guy went for me while Mark was given a great big blow job with my lips. This was really wild. I dig it having two big cocks to work on. Ever done anything like that?"

I avoided an answer by simply saying: "I'm not a woman."

She laughed, but left it there, merely winking seductively at me.

"What else do you want to know?"

"How was it you decided to move in here?"

"Well, after that swinging day of it, the others said I should rent an apartment. There was one open and they'd use their pull to get it for me, if I was interested. Boy, was I interested! You see, you become friendly with everybody real quick. No loneliness. No having to pick strangers up.

And most important there are no emotional demands made on you. It is easy to get a sex-party going on. Make a few phone calls, or simply make the pool-side scene and before you know it you're in some guy's pad or up in your own apartment. Maybe there are several couples with you. Maybe you've gone up with a couple of girls and a guy or a trio of guys, all for yourself. Though I dig relating to one man at a time there's something orgastically wonderful about having it with several big guns at once, if you dig?

"I've had the scene with two guys that way and I don't really want to rush into anything. And there is a very important point: only after I've really had a big blasting good time with a lot of guys will I be ready to know what kind of man I could stand living with for the rest of my life.

"You see, I've finally gotten to the point where I admit to one basic fact of life: the more guys you get on intimate terms with the more you know about what you want in a man. Once the whole bit of sex is out of the way then you can consider the very important item of do you have anything else going for you. They said—somebody, anyway—that people should date at least twenty members of the opposite sex before settling down to one for marriage. I think it goes further than that. The more sexual experience you get the better off you'll be. You'll know what the score really is.

"Both the guys I married should have been nothing but lovers—not husbands. Under those circumstances I wouldn't have...well, ended up divorced. That's the mistake so many young kids make. Getting married too soon to the wrong mates. Too many think that because they have a hot groin for somebody they are in love. Sex isn't love. And love isn't just sex. There's so much more to it.

"You know, if we could have more places like this—maybe a law saying that people can't get married until they have lived a little—in this kind of atmosphere—there wouldn't be so many hung-up kids. They'd learn what life is all about. And—"

"What do you think it is all about?"

"Learning what makes you tick and what you really need to find happiness. If there is a lot of wonderful, open, wild, free sex offered you don't get confused about the sex-thing and the love-thing. Then you're ready to consider what you want in life. What you are as a human being, sexually and emotionally and mentally."

"What do you consider yourself"

"Certainly not my sister or my folks. I'm not hung-up like any of them! I'm not interested in another damned foolish marriage for a long time. Until then I get a good chance to have a healthy sex-life. We are only young once, you know. And while I'm young and considered beautiful and desirable to men, I'm cumming with as many good-looking, long-lasting cocks as possible.

"Why shouldn't I? Why should I throw away a good thing? Soon enough I'll be old. And since I don't want to get married, why should it be necessary for me to be without a good healthy supply of sex? Dig? Grooving all the way. Riding the waves, as they take me, without worrying about what tomorrow will bring.

"I don't have to consider anything other than having a great time. I'm not lonely. I don't have to think about the shit world we live in with all its racial problems and political leaders being killed and wars that get us nowhere. I'm not bothered about being all by myself in front of a television set, watching a boring show. I don't have to worry about picking strangers up.

"We learn to know one another very quickly here at the apartment. We're almost family, in a way. A kind of small town for young singles who want thrills by the basketful without questions asked. Like that first experience I had with five other people. Just casual and thrilling orgasm, in any combination I might desire."

"Do you go for Lesbian relations?"

"No, that's where I draw the line for myself. But if other girls dig that, that's their business. I dig men's cocks and nothing more. Or less. I'm not about to be like my sister. She just might as well not exist. My folks? Hell, they are like most people of the older generation. To see my mother you wouldn't think a cock would melt in her mouth. To hear them talk about sex—even when they do—it sounds as if they think it is dirty or something. I'm bored to tears with those kinds of people.

"The kids that live here are on the ball. They are with it. Living in the present world, accepting it like things are—not trying to make things the way they should or might be. That's what the whole thing is all about, friend. Facing up to what the world is all about and grooving all the way. Just for the hell of it."

* * * * * * *

A little more was said, but most of it repeated much of what Gale had already said. I couldn't help feeling there was every reason to believe she was a woman who rebelled against society, against what her parents had taught her, against the world itself. I believe she felt sex was dirty, but wouldn't admit it to anybody—not even consciously. Her over-reaction about sex and about her open dislike for people like her sister and parents seemed just that: over-reaction. Yet regardless of everything, Gale seemed far happier than she might have been if living under different conditions.

I couldn't help wondering, after talking to her—and having talked to some others by then—if maybe a part of the more openness of the modern generations (especially those living in the apartments for singles only) is merely a desperate attempt to rattle society, to split with the older generation in the most bold and brazen way possible. In other words: rebel against authority. That in itself isn't wrong so much as fooling oneself into believing there are other reasons.

I felt that Gale was just as hung-up as her sister, merely reacting in a different way. Which one is best for a person to pick—total refusal of sexual relations, or wild open acceptance of orgies, is probably a question each reader must make for themselves. Maybe for Gale the answer will come in time and she'll reach the point where it is possible to relate to human beings in a total fashion, not afraid to feel emotionally and to give of herself as a human being, not simply a human body.

Until that time I believe she is simply fooling herself into believing a different kind of mental fantasy about life and sex—one that is a reverse of that which her parents' generation has. At least she pointed out there is more honesty in telling the truth about what you are doing rather than claiming that sex isn't nice, yet enjoying it behind locked bedroom doors—and probably feeling guilty about it. At least people like Gale are attempting to break out of the mold their parents created. It is a step in the right direction.

CHAPTER THREE

JERRY

He is in his middle twenties and is the kind of guy who will probably look young for quite a few years to come. Curly, short dark hair, handsome features and a trim body. He's the kind of guy a lot of women go for, especially the ones who want sex without attachments. They know instinctively he'll take them and leave them.

Jerry told me in the first minutes of our interview that this was the first time in his life he'd had a chance to really swing with anything but prostitutes.

"I got started later than most guys. It was all my own fault. It took me some time to realize that most girls are nothing but cute little cunts. A guy grows up thinking of women like—well, kind of sisters. I never had a sister, but I had cousins of the female sex. Most of them were sort of small town types. They got married fairly young. One, a few years older than me already has a couple of kids and I guess they'll have a blasted bunch before they're too old enough to function sexually. They don't believe in birth control for religious reasons—though they don't belong to that Roman church—the big church that is pushing everybody to have as many babies as they can—and overpopulate the world! I refuse to even speak that church's name. I don't believe we should consider sex as something created by a God simply to give birth to children. If that was true, then each and every screw-job would cause a child to be born. Or we wouldn't be so hot to make the fucking scene just because it damned well gives us pleasure. Sex is fun and I think people should have a lot of fun and games with one another!"

"You sound like you don't like children," I probed carefully.

"Hell, I just love little girls of all ages. Though I wouldn't screw some broad who was underage. Not any more, that is. I've had young flesh. But I was underage, too. That makes it different. If I did a thing like that, now, at my age, I'd be thrown into the box with bars on it. Nothing is worth that. I know some guys that just dig it the most to pop a girl's cherry. And if you want a girl who is really passionate and want to pop a cherry you have to look for ones about fifteen or younger. The others usually are sexually cold. If a girl doesn't have her cherry popped by then, there's something wrong with her sexual urges. That's what they say...well...not for me!"

"You really believe that?"

"Well, it certainly seems to be true. Look at the girls around here. Gale is the only one I know who took longer. But I guess she has had her hang-ups. She sure made up for lost time!

"Still, even she points the way—meaning, she was under age when she had her cherry banged in. Anybody with a hot groin will end up with at least some experience before they are eighteen. I hate to admit it, I almost didn't make it.

"I was sixteen when I had me my first piece of ass. With a girl down the block. We dated some and one night she just came out and asked if I'd like to do it to her. I was bombed out by that. I couldn't believe my ears!

"I mean, like she comes right out and says: 'How about doing it to me?' Today it would probably be worded more bluntly, like, 'Want to fuck me?' And I've had a couple of girls come out and say that, too! It is a crazy world today and anybody not with it—well, I feel damned sorry for them. They're damned fools. Like people have groins that should be worked—given a good working out! Otherwise your sex juices dry all up. I read that somewhere. When a girl or man doesn't have a chance to screw they literally dry up, sexually!"

"You believe that?"

"Face the facts! The more sex you get the more you want. When you're turned on, man, you're blowing full blast. If you're turned off—forget it! Kids who get married without having experienced a sexual orgasm with each other are out for trouble. They'll have a hell of a honeymoon—the girl disappointed and the man frustrated! I know what I'm talking about. Had a bad time of it."

"How's that?"

"Well, take that first girl. She just offers her cute little pussy. I'd never done it with a girl and didn't know really how to handle matters. Well, I mean, no experience. Everybody knows that a guy sticks himself in a girl. Gee hell, when I first heard about that I almost vomited. But I was too young to even have the ability to get a hard on. So...."

He shrugged his shoulders.

"So here we are in the car and the girl is screw-happy and telling me she wants me to do it to her. So, I'm not dumb. I'd played jerk-off with myself long enough to know what it felt like to have a cum. I knew I was supposed to stick myself inside a girl's pussy and jerk myself in and out—and I figured that was going to feel damned good!"

"Did it?"

"Feel good? Well, let me tell you. She's coming on strong and sexy. We're necking real hot and heavy. Like she's already let me give those boobs of hers a good working over with my hand. She's moaning something wild!

Likes her titties squeezed and fondled. They were big for a girl like her—about a year younger than me. Funny thing, I saw her a couple years back—last year, come to think of it—and she'd lost her figure. Like what was great at the younger age had turned to fat, fat and more fat. Big over-breasted cow with fat hips and fat stomach and fat arms. I guess a fat pussy, too. What her husband has to go through!"

He laughed as if that was some kind of joke, then lighted a cigarette. "Well, there we were, panting and wanting and she has just finished sucking my tongue so hard into her mouth that I thought it would come out by the roots. And I'm hard! I'll tell you, hard, but big and hard all over. My prick was tingling hot and hurting against my pants. The kiss breaks and she comes out with: 'Let's do it!' I started trembling all over the place. I couldn't believe it. I was a little frightened but so hot I didn't care.

"See, as it turns out, she'd fucked before; knew what to do. I guess it was a help in a way. Always do it with an experienced chick first time around. Right?"

"Helps to have a good teacher," I admitted, since the silence demanded some kind of response.

"So, she just rolls up her sweater. Like, rolling it up over her bra.

"Something erotic as hell when a girl does kind of thing. She rolled it up over her bra, that's all. Reached around and undid the bra and out flung her boobs. She peeled the bra up against the sweater and then thrust out her chest real proud. Grinning, looking up into my eyes as if it was something great to expose herself in that way.

"I said: 'Don't you want to take that stuff completely off?'

"She kind of giggled and announced: 'They're naked enough so you can suck them!'

"Boy that turned me on, really hot. They were plump,

supple, firm balls of meaty flesh with big over-size nipples and that rosy area around them was two—hell, maybe three—inches across. More than enough to fill my mouth with. I'd never sucked tits before, but the idea was so appealing that I found myself smothered against one breast, sucking her nipple like I was trying to draw milk from it. She held my head with her hands, fingers curled around to the back of my neck. They caressed and squeezed, then moved me to the other breast. Back and forth from one to the other, making pleasure sounds with her big lips. I was so hot sucking that tittie I almost came in my pants. Damned if I wasn't already wet by the time she pulled me away and said it was time for me to show her something. Like a silly ass I asked what she meant and she gigglingly reached out and touched my pants, where an erection was pressing against the cloth. That touch made my hot prick twitch with a cum.

"I was embarrassed when she opened my fly and saw I had already shot my juice. But it didn't stop her. She made gushing sounds with her mouth and gripped my cock with one hand around the shaft and palmed the tip saying how nice and juicy I was...real pleased. I wondered if she knew what had happened—like I'd cum.

"Her actions were pretty bold and sophisticated for any girl. Woman, for that matter. But the contact of her fingers working on my gun was so damned thrilling that I started responding. She continued to giggle and said 'You already got all wet because of me! And you're getting big again. Oh, its so nice and hot and big.' I was getting hard, too, by then. She had been playing with me for some minutes, of course, before I really began responding. It was the first time any girl—hell, anybody—had touched me that way. And I was young and juiced up enough—because never having done my bit before—that I could respond again. But I was embarrassed as hell.

"Finally when I was hard, she released me, lifted up

her skirt, gathering it around her waist, pulled down her panties and slipped them off her legs. She said something about not being able to wait until I got in her. Well, at the time I didn't know what was expected, didn't even know a girl gets moist when she's fully aroused or that her lips of love swell. She knew—but apparently didn't care and probably figured I knew what to do.

"Well, I managed to get myself between her parted thighs and instead of attempting to stimulate her with my cock-end and shaft, tried to force my way into the chambers of heavenly pleasure that my whole groin was almost orgastically over-stimulated to explore. Like, I couldn't get in fast enough. I tried, forcing my way past the doors, so to speak. It was a real tight squeeze. I was hard as hell and stiff to cum. The instant I managed to force my way an inch into her I climaxed and went down to limp almost immediately.

"She was furious, as you can guess. I figured it was a fizzle and over with. She demanded I do something to her, like tonguing what I'd wanted to enter or finger her. I was so embarrassed and sick that I ended up fingering her to orgasm, because she was there pleading that I do something. She figured I'd got my cum and she wanted hers. I remember her saying something like: 'Hell, for God's sake, do something, I need it bad.'

"Under such circumstances, today, I wouldn't have withdrawn from her pussy, but rammed myself the rest of the way in and started working myself around inside her until I got me another big fat erection."

"Did you see her again after that?"

"Are you kidding? Even if she would have let me...I was too embarrassed and sick to face her. I'd made an ass of myself, real ass and promised never, never to do that again as long as I lived.

"Not sex. Making an ass out of myself. I determined to get experience, but not with girls I knew. It took me some days to come to the conclusion that the best answer would be a whore. But here I was a kid and didn't know how to go around it. A friend of mine had an older brother and I managed to get talking to him about girls and then sex and then when he said he'd had himself a prostitute I asked what it was like.

"He told me she went down on him, real good and then when he was up like a rock let him enter her. Claimed it was better than with a date, because they were willing to do anything you demanded—for pay! Of course! He pointed out that with a girl you might not get any, ever— and not for some time at great expense and it usually wasn't as good! I learned he knew a girl willing to screw anything for twenty dollars. My next problem was getting twenty dollars.

"So I went to my dad and told him I needed twenty bucks and what could I do to earn it. He asked what I wanted it for and I said for something at school—like a project or something. He handed over a twenty-dollar bill and I felt like a bastard for lying. Later I told him the truth and—well, that's another part of the story.

"So I tell my buddy's brother what I want and he makes a call to the girl, even drove me over to her apartment—where she lived with her mother, who was out working. Once I was alone with her she asked if I had the money and told me to give it to her first. I asked how I would know she'd come across. And she said: 'Look kid, I have a reputation to uphold. If I don't please a guy the word will get around that I'm out to screw men, instead of letting them screw me. Okay?'

"After I gave her the bill, she started getting undressed and told me to do the same. I was pretty damned embarrassed. Then she took me into her bedroom, asked what I wanted so I tell her I want some experience. She laughed, knowingly, I guess and announced: 'I'll give you the kind of experience you want. Nothing like having me a virgin.'

Like an ass I said I'd done it with a girl. She grinned, but was smart enough not to make any wise crack.

"As she told me to get on the bed she promised: "I'll be sure to give you your money's worth, honey!' Well, I'll say one thing for this girl, she worked for the twenty. I guess she wasn't what you'd call a real professional whore, just a young woman making an easy fast buck doing something she found interesting work. I don't mean she got orgasm from her work—maybe she did, I don't know. Most don't. A very few do. It is a job and they are totally professional about it—emotionally detached. Just like going to an office and typing or filing. Though I wouldn't be surprised if this girl got started prostituting herself because she liked sex and figured it would be an interesting way to make enough easy money.

"I don't think I really gave her any great orgasm, though possibly she received some pleasure, considering her reactions and responses and what she later said about liking it when the guy wasn't experienced, because it gave her a kind of pleasure to be the dominant teacher.

"I've heard women tell me they enjoy it with a male virgin, psychologically, if he's any good at all. One said: 'Maybe like a man likes having a cherry to bomb out. I don't know. The young are eager and anxious. If you can get more than a couple of comes out of them it can be very satisfying, because somewhere along the line the guy is going to have enough control and you've worked yourself up quite a bit by then. Almost anything would give you a cum!' Well, something like that, anyway.

"In any case, this girl played with my penis with her hands and then gave it lip-service. Boy, feeling a woman's mouth around my cock, like that, for the first time, was something special!

"I never knew anything could feel so damned good!

"So warm and moist and active. Her lips kept moving up and down around my hard and her tongue danced a storm, seeming to hit all the exciting places—not missing a thing.

"Hell, it was better than my first experience with the young girl. I'd never been totally enveloped by a woman before—or anybody, for that matter! I ain't queer! You can bet on that!

"So, I just lay back arid bathed in the sensations her active mouth and tongue were dishing out.

"You know how it is. You lay back and this broad is giving you a real good working out with her mouth, tonguing you and blowing up a storm! You're in a kind of relaxed heaven. Plus under the right circumstances there's the double kick that the chick is kind of worshipping your penis. Makes you feel real great! Know what I mean?"

I merely nodded to give the required response.

"Well, there I was, lying on my back, getting myself the first real sexual experience in my life.

"She knew how to do it, too. Didn't get me so excited that I cum with her lips wrapped all around me. She didn't want me to fountain out an orgasm that way. Though she wasn't against letting such a thing happen. The guy who had brought me over said she'd done it all the way with him with her mouth.

"This girl, though, wanted me to get what I paid for. Experience. She said word of mouth was the only advertising she got and the better the word the more guys would come for what she had to sell. I've heard that kind of thing many times from whores."

"I take it you've tried quite a few."

"Wait! Just a while. I'll tell all. There's a hooker to this hooker." He grinned, amused by his own line. Then continued: "So, she's blowing a big number on my trumpet, a lot of lip and tongue work. I'm lying back and enjoying every blasted moment of it!

"Then suddenly her lips slowly pulled up to my crown and lifted away.

"I mentally kind of jarred. But she straddled me and started using her pussy-lips against my shaft, which was even wilder to me. I'd never realized that could feel so good. She didn't wait long, realizing I couldn't take that kind of torture very long. Suddenly I was in heaven, gripped by her hot, moist snatch, which she worked up and down on me with rapid, jerking motions, fairly sucking out my cum from my over-bloated dick. When I went off I thought I was going to shit at the same time. I thought my nerves were going to fly apart—or that in the last moment I did—and what a way to go, man!

"Well, the next thing I know she's wiping me with a wet wash rag until I was 'squeaky clean' as she put it. The way she cleaned me, kind of pulling on my limp penis with the warm rag wrapped around, was sensual and meant to be so. Because then she started mouthing me again until I got rock hard. We did it that time with me on top. She told me what to do in subtle ways. Like take it easy and move slower. She was nice about that. I only wish she'd been as clean about herself as she was with me.

"Like, see, she comes down with clap. Man was my buddy's friend in a panic. When I learned about it I went into such a panic I did the first smart thing in my life. I told dad the truth about what had happened with the twenty dollars and that the girl had clap. He gave me a real balling out. Partly about lying to him and mostly about getting into such a situation. First thing, he got me to a doctor. On the way back home that afternoon he announced that if I wanted to get sexual experience he would line me up with a real professional call-girl who was clean. In his business he had to know how to get call-girls in order to entertain clients.

"I won't bore you with the details. But he lined me up and said he'd take care of the bill. I guess the girl did it for free, because I can't see my dad handing out twenty-five to a hundred dollars for his son's sexual education. She was getting a lot of business through dad and probably considered it a good smart move to take good care of his son. I had myself more than a dozen lessons from this woman. When I got a job, during summer, I saved my money and started seeing this woman and others like her, whom she brought me into contact with. It went on like that for some time.

"But not until I started dating girls and learned about this place, did I really learn about sex and life and the way things are. In other words, for a long time I got my sexual thrills with whores and dating companionship with some of the girls in school—later at work. Then I learned that these girls were just as willing to screw—and cheaper, in the long run—as whores.

"See what I mean about this kind of thing being great!"

"I take it you aren't interested in developing anything serious with a girls."

"Oh, hell, at my age? You must be kidding! I want to live and see what it is all about! We only live once and anybody is a damned fool to screw-up their chances to have a great living experience while the action is there to grab. Like, people should grab life by the balls, with both hands! Swing—or as everybody is saying now, groove. Like ride along with what is happening and experience life the way it was meant to be experienced. Anything goes"

"You mean, here at the apartment."

"No. Everything but pot-parties. When that kind of thing starts to happen the owners jump all over the place. That is just about the only line they draw. No pot-parties. Hell, any person stupid enough to take pot would be...out of his mind in more than one way."

"Have you ever tried it?"

"No, and I don't plan on it. I feel it's enough to groove on girls, ride them like I'm the record needle and they're the record groves! Making beautiful music together. As far as booze, well, some people need something to loosen them up. A few drinks will make a shy sexy broad a little more willing to break free of her hang-ups. That's what we're all trying to do—break out of our hang-ups. I admit it, I've had some."

"What do you think they were?"

"Not understanding that most girls will put out! I guess that's it. They're just like the professionals, but more fun."

"Don't you think, maybe, it is simply that they're just like the men, having sexual and emotional needs?"

He thought for a moment, then said: "Sure. That's what I'm saying."

I didn't comment on his attitude, which I believed was a little bit rough on girls. He'd apparently grown up to believe girls should be pure until married and then realized they were just as human as men. As of this point he hadn't accepted the reality there was nothing wrong with a woman wanting to find love in a man's arms. He considered such girls much as he considered prostitutes. It wasn't the time to point this out to him. So I held back.

"You see," he continued, "I never realized how cheap and wild some girls can be. Like some of the things that have gone on here at the apartment. You wouldn't believe it. When I first came here I never knew there were girls who would go for getting together with more than one guy at a time. Some of these chicks will willingly blow one man while letting another stick her pussy. See what I mean? They're tramps. I sometimes wonder what the world is coming to." This last was said very seriously and thoughtfully. "Well, what I mean is simply, I dig this kind of operation where you can get all the hot cunt you want. But where are the nice girls who save it for the man they'll marry?"

"Every where you look. It's just that you have to look at women from the view-point that they are as human as you. They get lonely and they have sexual desires. If they aren't going to get married young why should they deny themselves a sex life?

"The well adjusted and emotionally mature will learn to develop a sex-life that fulfills their needs, without guilts. They will accept the fact that a man and woman need total a relationship. That can mean anything the two involved think it means. When both become active in sexual relations it becomes a more involved relating.

"But I don't think a guy should think of women as being tramps because they give themselves to a man. It is their nature to give. The man accepts their act of love—and should realize it is the greatest gift a woman can give—her body."

He shook his head from side to side and said: "Look, buddy; when a woman spreads her goodies around to any cock willing to fill her up...that isn't respectable—but it is one hell of a ball to have a girl like that. Each and every night, if you want. I don't have to worry about when or where I'll get my pussy. I get it on call, because there are a lot of girls here who are more than willing to climb into bed and have one hell of an orgy. It's great!"

"Would you marry any of these girls?"

"I never considered that one way or another. But as a quick answer, I'd say no. Yes, I'd say no."

"Don't you think you should get sex out of the way with the woman you marry?"

"I guess...I see what you mean there. Maybe."

"Then you've solved part of the problem. You can relate to her as a human being, a person—concern yourself on what else the two of you have to give to one another other than merely sexual relations."

He shrugged. "Hell, I'd rather not worry about all that kind of thing, right now. My concern right now is living to the hilt and getting as much experience with women as possible. I don't want to bother about tomorrow. It might have me fighting in a war that's immoral. So, don't bother me with such deep thoughts. Until I've found out what I want in life and been given a chance to know I can have a future, I'm not going to with anything other than grooving with as many broads as possible and this is the place to do just that!"

I considered him for a moment and then mentally sighed. It seemed that he had a long way to go before full maturity would hit him over the head. Until then, this was a perfect set-up for him. Because, as he said, there were plenty of girls at the apartment more than willing to serve up a sexual feast without any real efforts to go through the long process of dating.

His statements had proven one more point: *For Singles Only* meant that people could make up their own world, create their own adventure and thus discover through easy experience what it really is all about. His type of attitude fit into the immediate "world" he lived—the sex island apartments. I only hoped for his sake that he'd grow up and begin considering the women he slept with as human beings to be respected, not looked down upon as fast or cheap. The new morality has opened doors for both men and women and each must realize this in the light of self and mutual respect.

Being in the position to see and hear from both men and women, like I am, I realize that the women have respect for themselves, if they are mature enough to understand what the true meaning of life and living is all about. The others are tormented like this young man was; not sure what it really is all about and considering the others around him merely as play things for his pleasure.

CHAPTER FOUR

PEGGY

Peggy is twenty-two, a blonde with deep blue eyes and nicely shaped lips. Her figure is slender but sensual and there is a general look about her that makes a man think it would be a delight to plop into bed with this pretty little doll. Her manner is that of a woman who is part kitten and part sophisticated. She moves like a woman trying to consciously attract a man's attention. The way she holds a cigarette can be suggestive, especially when she places it between her lips. She'd blow smoke as if blowing a kiss and look at you with those wide eyes as if naughty thoughts were being subtly, suggested to you.

She is, visibly, a kind of subtle tease. It is surface—as is her sex-life and verbal attitudes. Only when you hit a nerve does all the slickness and the real, more tormented and confused Peggy surface. The outer personality she gives public display is a cover-up for deep inner doubts about herself and the world she lives and the sexual activities she indulges in.

We sat in her living room on the sofa, coffee on the table in front of us. She offered me cigarettes, but lighted it herself and then placed it between my lips. It was an intimate, seductive move. Though nothing happened between us of a sexual nature, it would have been quite easy to share a bed with her—if that had been my desire. It would never have taken place, however, since I worked for information not seduction. Thus my questions led down a different and more revealing pathway.

"Everybody is talking about you and the book you're doing," was her opening remark after the tape-recorder started. "Just about everybody has really had a ball reading some of your books. If I didn't know better, it would be difficult to believe people actually said things like that for publication. Now that I know the truth—and in fact am becoming a subject for your current book—I realize why people will actually tell all. Knowing that my real name won't be used and realizing you aren't the kind of guy to get all shook-up over a few dirty words and detailed intimacies, the whole thing seems really exciting.

"I've never really talked to a writer before and I've never thought it would be possible to tell all the gory details of my sex-life—for publication, to boot!—to anybody alive. Oh, sure, I've talked up a storm with a guy I'm...well, the word is screwing. But that's in the context of sex. You can say all kinds of things to guys who are turned on with you. And, to be frank, when you've been with some guys at one of those wild—really wild—parties that take place, where everybody is down nude screwing and fingering each other in front of everybody else...well, you take a different attitude. Like, if you've been jerking off one guy and then sucking on another at the same time while a third is fingering or kissing your sex heaven or maybe dicking you up good—it seems kind of silly to put on a false front.

"Then, of course, somewhere along the way people start using all those orgasmic words and it turns you on. Boy, when a guy says, 'You're jerking my cock good!' or half sobs, 'your pussy is really great around my prick' while you're screwing silly, it turns on the sex juices to pulsing blast. It makes the sex even more orgasmic. If a dirty word is used at the right time it really works wonders.

"Looking at a guy's big cock, hard and hot and having him say, 'That sexy body of yours made me that way!' or 'See what your pussy does to me?' you really get a charge. It makes you tingle all over, especially down between your legs where all those sex-nerves are screaming to be used."

She took a break to breathe, I guess. Then continues, saying, "I've done some crazy wild things since I've lived here. It really opened my eyes about how things really are. I mean, it would never have occurred to me that a girl could have a great time balling it with more than one man. I've done it with several guys at once, you know."

"How do you feel about that, Peggy?"

"At first I didn't think I liked the idea. But when it happened...well, I just went crazy. It was at one of the first parties I went to here. The conversation got going about different ways people could do it and one girl came right out and said she dug blowing one guy while another was screwing her snatch. Then somebody said that was a great idea and another said something like, how many guys could one girl service at once. The whole conversation heated all of us up, you can bet your orgasms on that!

"We started trying to think how many ways a girl could do it. Well, you can blow a guy, get one in your rear, you can jerk some guy off, and you can have one screwing your snatch. We decided the best combination for a girl to get the most out of it would probably be going down on one guy while another screwed her snatch and then she could play and jerk off two other hard-ons—one for each hand. The idea was shocking to me at first, but when one girl offered to give it a try and there were more than four guys willing to go along with her—right in front of us... well, if you watch a thing like that it is going to turn you on or off. Well, I'm no prude. You can bet on that. And it really made me juice up something painful. There's something wild about watching something like that. Ever done it? I mean see such a thing?"

"Well, I guess everybody has seek—"

She broke in a laughingly. "I was so embarrassed in the beginning. But I couldn't get eyes off all those four cocks dangling. The girl stripped and lay on her back in the middle of the room. One guy straddled her head and she played with him until his cock was hard and she could take it with her lips and mouth. What a wild thing seeing a girl run her tongue along the crown of a man's hard prick.

"I found myself getting excited. Then when another guy started on her pussy, while she used her hands on the other two, who lay down beside her in such a position that it was easy for her to reach between their legs—I thought how I orgasmic it must feel.

"I suddenly wanted to be her. I felt terribly and finally couldn't help myself any longer. Seeing her do that, being the center of attention with all those men, I couldn't stand it any longer and finally stood, started getting undressed and announcing I was more than willing to take on four other guys. There were plenty of guys there who jumped at the chance. It was a big party. We were the only two girls to put on a show in public like that, though.

"I've always dug using my mouth. I dig sucking on a man, all over. Especially dig a hard prick. There's something great and wonderful about feeling a man around your lips, filling my mouth. So big and hard and hot and softly covered.

"And responsive. A man is really responsive and my lips are highly sensitive. I just keep thinking that I'm doing this to the guy. And I get all turned on to go with the best damned style possible.

"A woman who knows how to use her tongue on a man can get some real great results. I've had me some guys that would last for a real long time. I try to make it last. Like when a man is getting to the point where he might burst loose with a big one, I back off enough to let him simmer down. I like to give a guy all the thrills I can. The longer it lasts the more fun it is all around. But I would imagine you know what I'm talking about."

"Do you like having a man perform cunnilingus on you?"

"What?" Her face screwed up in a puzzled frown.

"Go down on you with their lips," I offered.

She grinned wide, moistened her lips with the point of her tongue. "Oh, that can be great. Especially when I'm going big guns on him. But that's something else. You see, when a good pair of lips and an expert tongue is doing me up good, I get so damned orgasmic that I can't take my time. I just have to almost devour the man. It never lasts too long like that with me. I just can't turn off. I get all excited and start coming fast and I make the guy come with me. It is orgasmic!

"But what I was talking about was when I'm down on a man and using all the tricks I know to keep it going for a long, long session. Men like my kind of lip service and I'm proud that I'm so good at it. I've had guys come right out and say they'd heard how great I was and would I be willing to do it with them, too."

"What is your reaction?"

"How's that?"

"About having guys talk about you—telling others."

"Oh, at first I didn't dig that at all. But once I got into the swing of things here I realized it was the best thing in the world. Lip service from one man to the other gets me all the guys I want, when I want one. I'm very popular, because the guys know I want to make them it real good. I get all orgasmic inside knowing I'm doing such a good job on them. Having a prick come in my mouth, feeling it belching, jerking…oh, that's heaven!

"At first I was furious. But the guy gave it to me straight, saying: 'What's with you? They aren't talking behind your back—only saying that Peggy is really a great woman who wants her lovers to enjoy themselves to the fullest. They're complimenting you.' Before I thought it was kind of making out that I was cheap and easy. That's one thing I don't want people to think about me. You understand that, don't you?"

"Yes."

"No girl wants to be thought of as being cheap. It is different being willing to give as much as you get—pleasure, that is—but another to feel the guys think you're just an easy lay. I'd hate myself if I believe the guys thought that of me. I'm not a slut. I simply want to be a good lover. After all, they are giving me so much pleasure with their beautiful hard pricks that I want to return it. Oh, I just think it is wonderful to be given a man's hard prick to play with and then when it enters my...snatch...well, I get such a great amount of pleasure. I just love being screwed by a good lover. They don't know what it does to a girl. If they only know they'd believe we should pay them for the pleasure. So I just can't help trying to pay them back by letting them know how much I just love what they do to me.

"So that first time when the other girl was getting herself four big hard-ons to work on, I just couldn't control my own desire to do just the same thing. Watching the way she ran her tongue along the one guy's prick and the way her fingers and hands were playing with the two other guys, while the forth was sticking her up good...all I could think of was how great it must feel to have all that male meat giving it to you—responding to you! So I stripped and lay down on the floor a few yards away from her and guys took their place, automatically.

"First I had this big one over my lips and I couldn't control myself. My lips parted and I lifted up to cover that meaty cock. Oh, I trembled all over. Then my hands were eagerly searching for and finding two other big cocks that thrust eagerly into my grip. I was trembling to the feel of three pricks at once. Then when another guy lowered himself between my legs, rubbing his hard against my snatch I kind of went crazy.

"Before I knew it my snatch had snatched up one big meaty prick and was rapidly jerking up and down on it as fast as my hands were jerking on the ones in their grip. My mouth was frantically devouring the forth big hard and I was simply out of my mind in orgasmic pleasure. It was wild. I came fast and came fast and came as I felt the orgasms one after another respond to my acts of crazed passion.

"I was so turned on that I didn't even realize a new prick had entered my snatch. The other guys disappeared and there was this guy leaning over me, arms at my side and I just curled up around him, legs clutched about his, my arms almost clawing on his back. We screwed each other silly. I got at least two comes before he climaxed inside me. I couldn't let him go and he started swelling up hard inside my snatch and then I was jerking up and down on his big fat prick until it came again inside me. Then I fell back on the floor, exhausted, breathing hard, totally spent out as they say. "I'd never experienced such a thing before."

"What was your reaction later to what you'd done?"

"What do you mean?"

Her face shaded defensively and the tone of her voice was guarded.

"How'd you feel about what you had done later? After the pleasure and release had subsided?"

"Well, I was pretty knocked out, for one thing. And by the time I had recovered enough to dress and have a good strong drink and cigarette everybody was saying what a great, terrific show I'd put on. The girls got me aside and wanted to know how it felt and all I could say was that it was orgasmic. Everybody was making a fuss over me and all the guys were more than anxious to have a piece of my kind of action. They really knew I was a turned on girl who could take on any kind of sexual situation.

"I was a hit from then on."

"You said that you'd hesitated to do such a thing before—that the idea shocked you somewhat. How'd you feel the next day about what you'd done?"

The look on her face revealed that I'd hit a nerve. I couldn't help feeling there was an undercurrent of guilt about what she'd done. At least I was interested to discover what her attitude about her sex-show was once she'd had a chance to consider her actions in cold-blood. Her response surely revealed that while the words that told the story seemed to hold no guilt, there was, under the surface brazen attitude an inner confusion about such actions.

"I guess you're trying to make me say I felt guilty or something," she snapped back angrily.

"No, not at all. I'm just interested in your actions, because of what you said had been your first feelings about such public, multiple sexual acts."

"Well, for your information, I dug it. The next morning I lay in bed and thought how great it was to fuck more than one man and how much more orgasmic it had been to do it in public, like I'd done! I'd been a hit! Everybody thought I was great! I had turned on and had myself an orgasmic time and I couldn't wait to have me another session with more than one guy at once. I was thrilled silly and cut loose of all hang-ups.

"All I could think of was getting me a couple of big fat pricks to screw silly. I wanted to have me a fucking good time with two or more pricks at once. I kept thinking how great it had been jerking off two guys at once while fucking one in my cunt and blowing another with my mouth. I trembled all over thinking about what I'd done and wanting to do it again. And my pussy, oh, it burned. I was fingering myself without even realizing. I was just so hot!

Right then. I couldn't stand the idea of lying in bed and thinking about how great it had been rather than doing it some more like that."

"So what did you do?"

"What came naturally. I got my robe on, went to the phone and called up one of the guys I'd screwed that way the night before, asking him over. I told him to bring a couple of other guys because I dug what had happened the night before and I wanted to do it that way right now, again. So...he came over with two other dicks and I screwed all afternoon with them. I even took one in my rear while blowing another. The third had been bombed out by my pussy fucking so he was resting.

"By the time the three of us were finished, this guy was ready to let me blow him to a hard—which he used in my still hot pussy...and it was really burning hot. I couldn't get me enough male orgasms that day. I've never been turned on like that before in my life!"

"What do you think caused you to be so turned on?"

"Because it had felt so damned delicious—I wanted more."

"Have you been turned on like that since then?"

"Several times, but not quite as wild. Like the other day I had Bill and Roger over and we had a real good threesome. I was lonely and depressed and I wanted to keep from thinking about anything."

"What were you thinking about?"

"Mostly home. Family. I get that way. You know I came from back East and went to college out here. Then I got a job with an insurance firm. I'd been dating a guy who was screwing me hot and heavy. He was married. I'd never had a married cock before. I started dating him before I knew he was married. Then one night he suggested we go to a motel and I went. I'd been had before that. I thought I was in love with him. Later I learned he was married. But I continued dating him. That all happened in college. I guess I simply wanted to stay with him, no matter what it cost.

"So when I finished school, I got a job at the place he worked. We continued the affair for some months and then stopped when I became convinced he wasn't going to marry me at all. So...I stayed on, learning about this place from some friends I'd known in college. After breaking up with this guy I needed a really good sexual escape. I didn't want to think.

"But when I do start thinking about things, the way they used to be, I get sad and lonely and I'll get me some big cocks to keep me busy so I don't think about home."

"Why don't you want to think about home?"

"Oh, you don't know what it was like. My family is really prudish. Oh, if they knew I was fucking men like I do...they'd disown me. That's why I don't dare go back. I couldn't live in that small town without screwing men and everybody would know what was happening and I couldn't live with my family knowing what I was doing. My brother got married as a virgin. My sister did the same. My mother and father were virgins on their wedding-night. That's the way it is with them.

"There's nothing more terrible than coming from a family of hard nosed prudes. I don't know if you can understand that or not. But...you grow up thinking sex is dirty or something and when you learn what it is really all about it is quite a shock. Do you have any idea what I'm trying to say?"

"It is a problem everybody has to face, one time or another," I offered casually enough. "The world most of us grew up in was pretty much different than the one we're living in now. Not that sex wasn't going on, just that people simply refused to admit the truth about their activities. Not until the last couple of decades have people been forced to admit what they were doing had been doing for centuries. Wife swapping isn't new. Sleeping around with a lot of men—or women—isn't new.

"In the twenties a lot of changes took place, but they were kept, to some extent, quiet. Everybody knew what was going on, but it wasn't shouted all over the place. It was usually still considered wicked for a woman to admit publicly that she actually liked sex. That's because her mother usually didn't admit in public that sex was for anything other than having babies and doing the wifely duty.

"Because of our culture it was thought that women weren't supposed to like sex and if they did—they might be whores. That's because most men didn't take the time to make their wives like it or they felt that because their mother weren't supposed to have liked sex, their wives weren't supposed to like it. Women publicly claimed to be 'forcing' themselves to do what was expected of them. Their husbands would many times seek prostitutes to satisfy their sexual cravings with women who were admittedly more willing to do anything a man paid them to do. It was much easier.

"In the twenties women began getting their rights, and began drinking, and that made it easier to seduce them. The girl could say oh, it was the drinks. I couldn't help myself. I didn't know what was going on. And it did feel good, after all. It broke the ice. But most of that ice was behind the bedroom doors. It wasn't necessarily admitted in public, and certainly *not* to children. So children grew up with the same guilts about sex their parents had felt.

"Now that people are admitting that sex is fun and realizing that other people are doing a lot of really surprising things—like those key-clubs you heard about in the fifties, where you slept with the women whose key you picked up—then everybody stopped acting like they wouldn't of enjoying sex. They started to admit publicly that sex was fun. And now we have a generation that is saying that sex if fun and should be and we don't have to save it merely for having children because of the birth control pills. And other methods.

"There is far more openness about sex nowadays. It is healthy in that the guilts have a chance to be dealt with openly and not suppressed. The secret, I believe, is understanding what the guilts are and getting them out of the way so we can function as adult, mature human beings, relating to members of the opposite sex in an honest and open manner.

"In answer to your question, yes, I do understand what it is like to grow up having been fed a lot of lies that have to be handled within oneself and done away with. We all must learn to be honest with ourselves and admit that there is nothing wrong with having sexual feelings and relating to members of the opposite sex in a normal and healthy manner. Once we accept this, we are on the road to developing a healthy attitude about life in general and about ourselves and our relationship with others.

"This is not to say that people don't find a fully satisfying love-life within the bond of marriage. It is simply to point out there are as many possible choices a person can have, depending on where they grew up, what the culture permits and under what conditions they live. What's important is understand our inner selves, and our needs and learn to satisfy them as fully as possible. We all need to come to terms with our moral codes and our physical needs and to do so within the context of the culture we live in."

I stopped there to light a cigarette.

She grinned, said: "You really let out a mouthful, didn't you?"

I nodded, then suggested: "Why don't you continue, tell me about your family. How was it back home when you were a teen-ager."

"Pretty horrid. I didn't get my cherry knocked until I came here to college. Up to that time I believed I should save it for my husband.

had to do the same with my date. When he opened
I dropped him and started fondling and using my
on his prick until it got hard and large, then I was
use my lips like suction cups on his shaft. He cra-
y head with his hands, moaning in pleasure. It was
hell!

, I know she probably had had a mother who really
her the tricks. Boy, it was wild thinking about a
r doing such a thing, but she was totally unhung. All
ok place just about the time I met the married guy.
nd, well, things have changed since then. Some-
I wonder...well, when I get lonely I start thinking
how my folks would—well, think about what I've
doing and...sometimes I get...get terribly depressed
then I do—"
he suddenly broke off, her lips were trembling and
ropped her eyes to the floor.
...I...sometimes think maybe—what have I, well,
know, what have I...become? Her voice was choked
could see tears running down her cheeks. Abruptly
ooked up at me, tormented: "I feel so cheap. The
s—I told...you...I've done! My folks...would—" She
enly broke down sobbing, shaking.
moved close to her and slipped an arm around her
lders. She clutched to me like a little child, crying,
ing, and trembling. I tried to comfort her by saying
wasn't any reason to hate herself or feel guilty.
This continued for several minutes before she gained
rol of herself. Finally Peggy pulled away and wiping
eyes asked: "Do you really think there's nothing
ng with me? I mean, the kind of life I've lived."
"Everybody has to find out what they want to be. No-
y has a right to pass moral judgments upon others.
h person has to live their own life, Peggy, and make
kind of adjustments that will give them a full rich exis-
ce. Sex and love are two very important things in life.

"That's the way I was brought up. And the folks always said things like don't touch yourself down there —as
if 'there' were something I horribly dirty little hole filled
with horrid germs that would turn you into a witch. I've
talked to other kids around the apartment and some of
them have the same irritation about the way our folks generation was so damned hung-up. At least they could have
said, you shouldn't touch your vagina or penis. Use the
medical terms. But, then, in the first place, I wonder if
there is really anything wrong with touching yourself—I
mean, rubbing out a come against your groin?"

"Masturbation is a normal part of teenage life. I don't
believe there is anything wrong with it. In fact this is the
only real outlet young teenagers are given. Their bodies
are highly erotic and hungry for sexual experience and society says they shouldn't have sexual contact with one another. And, in reality, they shouldn't until they are old
enough to support the results of their mistakes."

"You really come on honest, don't you? I've never
talked like this with a guy before. Well, I would have been
embarrassed to admit this to a guy I hadn't fucked around
with. Even then I might not unless the conversation came
around to playing with yourself. But I beat up a storm in
bed at nights. I couldn't help myself. I just had to rub a
come. It was terrible. Now I know what I really needed. I
wanted me a big fat prick."

"How old were you when you had your first lover?"

"Lover?" She laughed. "It wasn't quite like that. You
see, I came to college at the age of eighteen, a prudish
messed-up virgin. The girls put me straight in a few
weeks. You know how it is at dorms. They all talk about
their dates and then you learn there are some girls who
really did have it with men. The older ones would back
their stories by showing you a diaphragm or birth control
pills.

"One girl was the daughter of a doctor who gave her

the pills because he didn't want her to get pregnant. We thought that was wild. But she explained that her father had made it clear he didn't expect her to go around sleeping with every guy she dated. The fact was she screwed less than most girls. She was very selective and dated one guy at a time and didn't sleep with all those guys. Just the special ones she really cared a lot about and was turned on by.

"But there was this other girl who had a diaphragm who got me on the ball. She was a real swinging one and it wasn't long before I knew she wasn't all talk. She told me it was foolish for a girl to be so damned hung-up. She said that her mother had helped her get a man for the first time, in fact was in the same room telling her what to do. Now that was a bit wild, if you ask me. But…well….

"They got a guy who was willing to be a subject. Her mother showed her how to blow a man, even to correcting her—taking her place.

"That was wild to hear about!

"She told me in real detail. Maybe part of it was… well, blown up a little, but I couldn't help believing her. You see, her mother was long divorced and apparently believed women should like sex and should know how best to please a man. So, when her daughter got old enough she started giving her a sex education. I couldn't go for that kind of thing from my parents, but…this sure was wild!

"First, just the facts of life, but not just like the birds and bees. She told her all about sex and what men liked to have done to them and what a woman liked to have done to her; and what men and women did together and why— of course, over the years. I mean, her mother didn't tell her all that all at once. Just a little 'be here' and a little bit 'more there'.

"But by the time this girl was about sixteen her mother had given her a full course and they got a guy to their house and had a sex lesson that taught her everything, but

everything! Her mother had traine[ ] wasn't any embarrassment. The gu[ ] joying himself. Two women, a m[ ] and a young, young thing wanting [ ] about. When this girl saw the man[ ] her mother started playing with his [ ] came sexually excited. She'd bee[ ] drinks first, so that probably helped.

"Anyway, she told me the sight [ ] ing and fondling the man's balls and[ ] She just simply had to feel what it wa[ ]

"Her mother explained how to do[ ] ter go to it. Before the day was up s[ ] under her mother's instructions and ha[ ] with him."

"You believed this?"

"Well, you had to know the girl, I s[ ] a guy, once. And she did everything[ ] done. We were on a double date and [ ] ment. I'd already had me a cock by [ ] come to think of it. And this evening w[ ] a double sex-date. We didn't screw in f[ ] but it got pretty hot and heavy before [ ] we go into the other room.

"He was already up my skirt with his[ ] been Frenching pretty hot and heavy. On[ ] site us, were this girl and the other guy[ ] open and was fondling his cock to hardne[ ]

"Then she fell down on her knees b[ ] between his legs—and started to Fren[ ] That's when my date suggested we spli[ ] chance to see more than her lips fold ar[ ] cock and slide down to take in a big portio[ ] shaft.

"Well, when we got into the bedroom[ ] seeing how she'd gotten her guy into her m[ ]

As a person grows older they learn that sex is not love and love without sex can be very painful and frustrating.

"But each of us has to discover what kind of sexual person we are—and this should be gotten out of the way before we get serious with somebody and get married. What you are experiencing right now is nothing more than a sense of guilt about doing things with men that your parents might not approve of. Once you stop trying to get their approval and get to the point where you accept yourself as the final authority of what you wish to do—in other words, become your own judge—you'll be a long way on the road to maturity—the real, long lasting maturity. If you find that you've been getting involved in sexual activities which are undesirable, then you should come to terms with it.

"All this is, of course, assuming that those you share intimacies are mature, consenting adults and nobody is being hurt...meaning, of course, consciously hurt against their will.

"There is nothing more wonderful than relating to one special person in a total manner. But until you find that person you'll have to come to terms with yourself and discover exactly what kind of person you are and what kind of person with whom you want to share your life. While you're searching for your real self it is quite normal that you'll experiment—in many ways and one of them are sexual.

"I believe you're only trying to discover what it is all about—and if the results of your exploration are bothering you that much, why not take a long step backwards and decide if this is truly what you want. If it is, stop feeling guilty about it. If it isn't—change, but don't feel guilty about what you've done in order to discover the real Peggy.

"In other words, everything we do in life is calculated to make us grow. We experience and learn. We shouldn't damn the mistakes, but rather bless them for what they taught us. Through mistakes, we learn.

"What you have been doing isn't in itself unusual, in that others haven't done it. But it isn't perverted unless you think it so and as long as this is simply your immediate way to self-discovery. Each person has to find out for themselves. I've talked to quite a few men and women who have found it sexually exciting to have intercourse while others were around.

"There are as many reasons for this as people. If those involved are all adults and consenting adults doing such things in private—in other words not in public where others who don't wish to be involved.

"Obviously it is not a healthy way to develop a sex life for marriage.

"An ideal marriage involves love of each other and a desire of sharing one another only with one another. At least this is the cultural norm. Though there are many couples who think nothing of swapping partners. That is their business. They are supposed to be mature enough to know what they want. If that's what they want, it's their own business, as long as they don't go around trying to force others who are unwilling to act in the same manner into doing the same thing.

"If you want to have a marriage with a man who wishes only to have you as a lover and nobody else, you'll obviously have to settle down and start on a new kind of approach to sex. But that will come in time.

"On the other hand, if you wish to continue having this kind of sexual experience, even in marriage, then you'll have to find a man who likes the same things. The important thing is that you discover what you really want and then go after it and don't damn the past. Learn from your mistakes, but don't feel guilty."

She sighed. "What makes me like it that way?"

"It thinks it is only your desire to over-react to your

"That's the way I was brought up. And the folks always said things like don't touch yourself down there —as if 'there' were something I horribly dirty little hole filled with horrid germs that would turn you into a witch. I've talked to other kids around the apartment and some of them have the same irritation about the way our folks generation was so damned hung-up. At least they could have said, you shouldn't touch your vagina or penis. Use the medical terms. But, then, in the first place, I wonder if there is really anything wrong with touching yourself—I mean, rubbing out a come against your groin?"

"Masturbation is a normal part of teenage life. I don't believe there is anything wrong with it. In fact this is the only real outlet young teenagers are given. Their bodies are highly erotic and hungry for sexual experience and society says they shouldn't have sexual contact with one another. And, in reality, they shouldn't until they are old enough to support the results of their mistakes."

"You really come on honest, don't you? I've never talked like this with a guy before. Well, I would have been embarrassed to admit this to a guy I hadn't fucked around with. Even then I might not unless the conversation came around to playing with yourself. But I beat up a storm in bed at nights. I couldn't help myself. I just had to rub a come. It was terrible. Now I know what I really needed. I wanted me a big fat prick."

"How old were you when you had your first lover?"

"Lover?" She laughed. "It wasn't quite like that. You see, I came to college at the age of eighteen, a prudish messed-up virgin. The girls put me straight in a few weeks. You know how it is at dorms. They all talk about their dates and then you learn there are some girls who really did have it with men. The older ones would back their stories by showing you a diaphragm or birth control pills.

"One girl was the daughter of a doctor who gave her

the pills because he didn't want her to get pregnant. We thought that was wild. But she explained that her father had made it clear he didn't expect her to go around sleeping with every guy she dated. The fact was she screwed less than most girls. She was very selective and dated one guy at a time and didn't sleep with all those guys. Just the special ones she really cared a lot about and was turned on by.

"But there was this other girl who had a diaphragm who got me on the ball. She was a real swinging one and it wasn't long before I knew she wasn't all talk. She told me it was foolish for a girl to be so damned hung-up. She said that her mother had helped her get a man for the first time, in fact was in the same room telling her what to do. Now that was a bit wild, if you ask me. But...well....

"They got a guy who was willing to be a subject. Her mother showed her how to blow a man, even to correcting her—taking her place.

"That was wild to hear about!

"She told me in real detail. Maybe part of it was... well, blown up a little, but I couldn't help believing her. You see, her mother was long divorced and apparently believed women should like sex and should know how best to please a man. So, when her daughter got old enough she started giving her a sex education. I couldn't go for that kind of thing from my parents, but...this sure was wild!

"First, just the facts of life, but not just like the birds and bees. She told her all about sex and what men liked to have done to them and what a woman liked to have done to her; and what men and women did together and why— of course, over the years. I mean, her mother didn't tell her all that all at once. Just a little 'be here' and a little bit 'more there'.

"But by the time this girl was about sixteen her mother had given her a full course and they got a guy to their house and had a sex lesson that taught her everything, but everything! Her mother had trained her so well that there wasn't any embarrassment. The guy, apparently, was enjoying himself. Two women, a mature, experienced one and a young, young thing wanting to learn what it was all about. When this girl saw the man naked and watched as her mother started playing with his balls and cock, she became sexually excited. She'd been given a couple of drinks first, so that probably helped.

"Anyway, she told me the sight of her mother squeezing and fondling the man's balls and prick was too much. She just simply had to feel what it was like.

"Her mother explained how to do it and let the daughter go to it. Before the day was up she'd blown the guy, under her mother's instructions and had sexual intercourse with him."

"You believed this?"

"Well, you had to know the girl, I saw her in action on a guy, once. And she did everything she told me she'd done. We were on a double date and at this guy's apartment. I'd already had me a cock by that time—several, come to think of it. And this evening was my first time on a double sex-date. We didn't screw in front of each other, but it got pretty hot and heavy before my date suggested we go into the other room.

"He was already up my skirt with his fingers and we'd been Frenching pretty hot and heavy. On the couch, opposite us, were this girl and the other guy. She had his fly open and was fondling his cock to hardness.

"Then she fell down on her knees before him—right between his legs—and started to French his hard-on. That's when my date suggested we split. I didn't get a chance to see more than her lips fold around his erected cock and slide down to take in a big portion of that bloated shaft.

"Well, when we got into the bedroom I was hot from seeing how she'd gotten her guy into her mouth like that. I simply had to do the same with my date. When he opened his fly I dropped him and started fondling and using my tongue on his prick until it got hard and large, then I was able to use my lips like suction cups on his shaft. He cradled my head with his hands, moaning in pleasure. It was sexy as hell!

"So, I know she probably had had a mother who really taught her the tricks. Boy, it was wild thinking about a mother doing such a thing, but she was totally unhung. All this took place just about the time I met the married guy.

"And, well, things have changed since then. Sometimes I wonder...well, when I get lonely I start thinking about how my folks would—well, think about what I've been doing and...sometimes I get...get terribly depressed and—then I do—"

She suddenly broke off, her lips were trembling and she dropped her eyes to the floor.

"I...I...sometimes think maybe—what have I, well, you know, what have I...become? Her voice was choked and I could see tears running down her cheeks. Abruptly she looked up at me, tormented: "I feel so cheap. The things—I told...you...I've done! My folks...would—" She suddenly broke down sobbing, shaking.

I moved close to her and slipped an arm around her shoulders. She clutched to me like a little child, crying, sobbing, and trembling. I tried to comfort her by saying there wasn't any reason to hate herself or feel guilty.

This continued for several minutes before she gained control of herself. Finally Peggy pulled away and wiping her eyes asked: "Do you really think there's nothing wrong with me? I mean, the kind of life I've lived."

"Everybody has to find out what they want to be. Nobody has a right to pass moral judgments upon others. Each person has to live their own life, Peggy, and make the kind of adjustments that will give them a full rich existence. Sex and love are two very important things in life.

upbringing. You are rebelling. Doing what you know your parents wouldn't like. Tell me the truth. What were your real, deep-down feelings the first morning, after you'd had those four men at the party?"

"I cried some. I was sick and depressed," she in a small voice. "I felt sick with shame and disgust.

"I guess...well, I felt like dying inside. I had to admit I'd done those things and that it had been great fun—I mean it all felt good sexually to me—but I was kind of shocked to realize...well, I could do such things. You know what I mean, I guess. Then I got to thinking since I'd done them it was too late to change that fact. So I accepted this—I had to. I couldn't escape what I'd already done. Then I got to thinking what my parents would think and...I wanted to run and hide and scream. I ended up— well maybe escaping?"

A small smile formed on her lips. "I guess I was escaping by calling the boys over. I didn't have to think about anything but orgasmic things. Maybe that's what I have been doing ever since."

I don't know if she resolved some of her conflicted feelings or stopped enjoying the kind of sexual experiments she had been involved with, but my hunch is that she was rebelling against parental messages still deeply imbedded into her mind.

Forgetting any moral bias, remaining non-judgmental, one can only say that given time Peggy will find her way to a satisfying solution which works for her.

That is, in the long run, the only real solution for all of us to discover. The road to ultimate happiness is a bumpy pathway through life, and we all end up stumbling and we all go through stages of self-discovery. And it is a hit and miss experience. The best any of us can hope for is more success than failure.

Peggy was a lovely person and hopefully she'll discover the satisfying life she richly deserves.

CHAPTER FIVE

RITA

Rita is what some men would call hefty, others would call her highly voluptuous. She has very large breasts, wide hips and meaty thighs. For a man who likes his women slender, Rita would seem too fat, though it isn't fat actually that pads her body. For a man who likes a real meaty woman, Rita's the girl. She is half-Mexican, half-Irish, with a little German and Russian thrown in for spice—as she puts it. Like many Latin girls she is broad-boned and carries her weight attractively. She developed breasts in her very early teens that were quite large by fourteen.

I saw a picture taken of her at that time. By nineteen she was a brimming sexual package. The picture showed a girl in a two piece bathing suit and the bust-line was blooming, bulging around the top of the suite with large rounded supple flesh. Her stomach was rounded, not as flat as some men like—though others find it highly attractive—dotted by a deeply tucked navel. Her hips wide, thighs firm and fully packed, flesh darkly tanned. Rita had a nude picture which she showed me, that revealed that her breasts, even today—she's twenty-five—are surprisingly firm and molded for a woman so greatly developed. The nipples are large and the areola darkly shaded and spread out. She showed this picture of herself with great delight and pride, then said there were others more erotic. She asked if I wanted to see them, while explaining that a boy-friend who was a camera bug had taken these pictures of her. She told me that it was kind of exciting posing in the nude and that she liked men to see the pictures.

I'd like to say my attitude about seeing the more "erotic" pictures was purely clinical—in order to get an insight into her attitudes about sex and what she believed to be "erotic." Naturally, this alone was purpose enough to see them. But being as human as the other guy, I can't deny some interest in seeing these pictures of what many men call a highly charged female package. Though I wouldn't have suggested that she show me the pictures under any circumstances. I also would be a liar if I implied being totally numb to the normal male interest in seeing so-called "erotic" pictures of an attractive, stacked female like Rita.

In any case the pictures were even more erotic than I expected. What would a woman call "erotic?" And what kind of pictures would a woman show a total stranger? More seductive poses? The first nude she had shown me had been a purely "artistic" picture of a woman's body—in this case hers. The other pictures were totally different. I expected something more along the lines of what is pub-lished in some of the "girlie" magazines—at worse the most far-out publications (though expected only some-thing like the average "girlie" magazine photo).

I didn't expect anything more than—at most pictures of her with legs spread and focal center on her vagina. What many people would call at least vulgar or out right dirty. And I didn't honestly expect anything that far out.

This is a general run-down on what she showed me, one at a time. All of the pictures were color shots, eight-by-ten-inch size. All were taken in her apartment.

The first showed her lying on the sofa, legs spread and

her hand caressing her vagina in such a way that it was obvious that one finger was penetrating her genitalia.

A man was standing beside the sofa, looking down, totally naked, positioned and angled in such a way that you could see his penis, in full erection. She had her lips open, tongue visibly moistening their surface. Her eyes were wide, looking at his penis with obvious lustful interest.

While showing me this, Rita said that most people think she was putting on a good show, "acting passionate excitement", but that in actual fact she was so voluptuously and erotically aroused that she really wanted to use her lips on his penis. The picture graphically illustrated this point.

The next photo showed her sitting on the sofa, the man standing between her parted knees. She was holding his hips with her hands and had his penis imbedded within her mouth. She told me that while the picture was being taken she was actually using her tongue on the bottom of his hard.

The third photo showed the two of them in a sixty-nine position, again giving an excellent view of the man's penis with her lips around it. She was on her back; he was straddled above her on the sofa. She explained that he was using the delayed shutter, and that there wasn't any cameraman around. If my memory serves me right (and it isn't a tape-recorder) she then said:

"Naturally I wouldn't do such a thing with a third person around. Though I've done such things as having more than one guy socking it to me at the same time. After this picture was taken we simply didn't stop going at one another. It was really great. We were exhausted. It was some time before we could take any more."

The next picture was showing them in a sixty-nine position again, but this time with Rita on top. Her fingers were wrapped around the man's penis at the base, holding it up. Her other hand apparently was cupping his testicles.

She had her lips around the crown of his erected shaft.

Another picture followed, showing her having sexual intercourse with the man. The angle was such that it was easy to see he was half penetrating her vagina. It was in the position, man on top.

There followed a picture with her on top, straddling his hips, but with no view of their sexual organs, since they were in full penetration, as she explained in a husky voice.

She quickly flipped through the other showing different positions. One was her sitting on the sofa, legs extended out and the man penetrating her vagina. Some of the photos show them in her bedroom doing much the same thing. She explained that it took quite a few weeks to get all these pictures.

Once she had shown me about twenty such photos she returned them to her bedroom while I set up the tape recorder. When she came back, the interview began in a general manner—just as conversation, much of which has been edited out.

But one of the first exchanges immediately upon her return was the following.

"How'd you like the pictures?" she asked, sitting down beside me, brushing her long black hair back over her shoulders. She wore a tight sweater and short skirt.

"They were very interesting."

"Oh, come on, didn't they excite you?"

"Were they supposed to?"

"I don't know. They usually excite men. I've never really shown a man those pictures unless I've had intercourse with him or plan on having it. But with you I figure it might be of interest to let you know about them and see them. Was it?"

"If you mean will it give me a better understanding about you and your attitudes concerning sex, naturally. But tell me how it was they happened to get taken."

"Oh, Dave, that's the guy in the pictures, is a camera

nut. We'd been...well, screwing for some months. We just got to talking about pictures and he asked if I would pose in the nude for him. That first picture I showed you was one he took of me. He tried to get me to pose for pictures to be sold to magazines, but I refused.

"Then we talked about such things and I said I didn't want strangers looking at my picture and wanting to jerk themselves off. That seems a little too far out. I said, too, that it wouldn't be fair for some guy to get an orgasm looking at my picture and me not getting the rewards. Though I happened to mention I wasn't against posing for erotic pictures, just for kicks and for myself and him. Then we got to talking and the conversation went something like this—to kind of round it out and give you the high points.

"He started saying it would be fun to take such pictures of me and I started saying it would be really fun. Then we started talking about what kind of erotic pictures. You see, he kind of probed, asking what I'd be willing to do...poses and things like that.

"I laughed and teased him a little by saying there wasn't any kind of pose I wouldn't be willing to make, just so it was for kicks and for us only. The more we talked the more the idea appealed to me. He was all for it. Then I started saying that there wasn't really anything I could think of that I wouldn't do before his camera.

"By then we were pretty drunk and had been necking a little and getting hot. After talking about sex and all that and knowing what kind of lover he was, I teased him by opening his fly and working my fingers into it until they found his prick. It got quick hard from my squeezes. We got him exposed and I started going down on him a little. Just sexual teases. We did things like that. We were still smoking and drinking.

"I had a cigarette in my hand as I lowered my head between his legs and smoked his cock a little. Then I laughed, took a drag of my cigarette and then a drag of his hard cock.

"We joked a little and then I said, I wouldn't even mind letting him take a picture of me doing that to him, but couldn't see how he could be holding the camera and letting me do this at the same time. He jumped at that idea, explaining how it could be done.

"We got so excited over the idea that we stopped sexing it up for a while, continuing to smoke and talk and drink—all the time his cock exposed—we didn't even think of re-zipping his fly. In fact we didn't even consider it one way or another. We were simply so turned on by the idea that we talked instead of me sexually teasing him to the point of intercourse. And then, of course, we planned on screwing each other silly before the night was up and had simply gotten as far as exposing his cock when the conversation flared up over taking really wild pictures.

"It was during this time that we decided just about every position we could take. In other words, all the pictures we finally took were all worked out that evening. Before long, though, we started acting out the possible positions and then got all wound up over what we were doing to one another. We were both naked by then. So...hell, when I get my lips around a man's cock it is hard to keep from drinking my fill of sexual thrills. And he's damned responsive in the sex department, too. We simply got erotically turned on. I guess you understand how it is."

"Then the idea was partly yours. The picture taking, that is," I offered.

"To be honest it was all kind of silly. Later we talked about it. He was trying to see if I would be willing to do such a thing—because he had always wanted to take such pictures, just for the hell of it. And I really thought the whole idea was wildly exciting. It simply took us some time before we were able to admit it to one another."

"How long ago was it? Apparently you were living here at the time."

"A couple of years ago, just after I'd moved in. This place, by the way, kind of turned me totally on, gave me the complete freedom to do anything I wanted to. Until then I simply rode along with the punches, you might say, and had natural affairs with guys I dated, but was living with my parents at the time. My folks are sophisticated. They'd done things like swapping with other couples. Though they never exposed either me or my sister to that. I only learned about such things much later.

"It was when my mother visited me here that she opened up a little for the first time about her own sexual life. It all came about fairly naturally. Again a long kind of probing until one door after another was opened and finally the whole house explored. She was smart enough to pretty much guess the kind of arrangement possible. She knew I was having lovers. There were times when she'd call up to say hello and a guy would be here—I mean like in the morning. We'd gotten to the point where she very naturally accepted my rights to a sex-life.

"That afternoon when she visited me the conversation just came around to the apartment and she commented that it was a damned shame they didn't have a place like this when she was young. After a while I was learning things about her I had never dreamed possible. I wasn't shocked, but in fact quite relieved to find out how human she is. It helped to make us better friends as adults.

"She didn't go into gory details about her sexual adventures but admitted to having had affairs before she met my father—and said he'd also had quite a few affairs before meeting her. She also admitted that they'd had an affair before getting married, though they didn't have to get married. They were modern for their time. My older sister June wasn't born until they'd been married for several years and they planned it that way. She told me that it had taken her a long time to accept her sexuality when she was a teenager and that she'd had her first affair at nineteen—

and felt guilty about it for months afterwards. Her attitude
was that our generation was lucky because they had a better chance not to be guilty about their sexual feelings and a
better chance to have affairs more openly than her generation had. That's why, mother explained, my sister and I
had been raised to be as well-adjusted as possible concerning matters of sex. And that was true. Like I said, she
didn't expose us to their sex-life, but at the same time gave
us a total sexual education as we grew up. Still, no matter
how sophisticated parents are with their kids, it is simply
impossible to have a really swinging sex-life while living
at home.

"There is the problem that if you stay out all night with
a man your folks might be worried you have been involved in an accident or something. And it is embarrassing
to call up and say, 'Mommy, I won't be home tonight, I'm
going to a motel with a guy and staying with him, so don't
worry!' So having a place of your own solves that problem. I was always sneaking into the house early in the
morning, trying not to wake up the folks, when I'd been to
a motel with a guy.

"One time, shortly before I moved out—in fact that
was why I finally made the decision to do so—my father
woke, saw it was five-thirty in the morning and realized
I'd just come home from my date. He didn't say anything
directly. I was over twenty-one. But it was embarrassing to
both of us. He tried to cover up by asking if I had a nice
time and I tried to cover-up by saying I'd simply been
talking with the guy and before I knew it the lies developed so far-out that I simply came out and shouted: 'Hell,
daddy, I'm old enough to do what ever I damned please.
My private life is my own. So I was with a guy! And it
isn't any of your business what we did. I'm sorry for lying.' I ran into my bedroom and slammed the door, and
fell on the bed, crying.

"After a while Dad came in and tried to comfort me,

saying he was sorry to have embarrassed me and that I was right about my private life being private and none of his business. We talked for a while and I said that maybe it was best I move out on my own. He tried to convince me it wasn't necessary, but I think he thought it would be best for my sake. Anyway, during the next few days I started looking for places to live. It took me quite some time to find this place.

"So, you see when I moved in I was free for the first time. I had a chance to experiment and do some things I'd never been able to do before. So the picture thing was one of the results. Actually I discovered this place because of him. He had a friend who was dating a girl who lived here." Rita shrugged and then said: "Well, anyway, that's the story of how I happened to get such a bang out of having those pictures taken. I didn't mean to go into such a long and involved story."

"Quite all right," I told her. "How old were you when you had your first sexual experience with a man?"

She laughed and said: "Eighteen. And that's quite a story. Maybe you'd like to hear it."

"Go ahead, if you wish."

"Well, my sister, being older, had sexual experiences by the time I was eighteen. My feelings had been to wait until I reached that age of consent for a woman. You know—it's all right for a girl of eighteen to have relations with a man. That's something I learned from my folks. They taught both my sister and me to have an intelligent attitude about sex. They never told us there was something wrong or dirty about it like so many other parents do. They simply tried to give us an attitude that would keep us from being foolish. They felt that when a person did something they should be old enough to be responsible for the results.

"I remember being told, 'don't go out sleeping around just to show off or for stupid kicks or because the gang thinks you should and you want to be in with the group. Don't do anything that can cause a result you can't deal with. When you are old enough to handle yourself and the responsibilities of your actions, that will be time enough.' I came to the conclusion that I would wait until I was eighteen and legally responsible before I'd have sexual intercourse with a man.

"I'd talked to my sister about that and she was pretty experienced by then. So, as it turned out she offered to line me up. We talked about sex and I said I really wouldn't mind learning how to do it. So we arranged a crazy thing. Really crazy!—I guess. But it made sense. She told me everything a woman could do to a guy and how to do it and had gone just about as far as she could without having some guy there to demonstrate by actions. In other words, it was like a teacher giving a course and getting to the point where in order to make everything perfectly clear it was necessary to take another big step—in this case, she needed a man there to actually show me what she was talking about.

"It didn't come all that fast. I should explain that we just got to a point where she said: 'Well, darling, that is just about as much as one can be told, the rest has to come from actual experience.' Then she started talking about her own experiences and then admitted to having had it with two guys at once and one time when she was rooming with another girl, they got a man up to their apartment and the two of them ended up having a three-way sexual thing.

"She'd done such a thing with several guys and was still socially going out with one who liked two women at once or any kind of sexual kick. Then suddenly she said: 'Hey, darling, he'd be more than willing to serve as a perfect subject to give you an advanced course. If you wished, I could even be there with you.'

"Well, the idea seemed crazy. It embarrassed me a little, but on the other hand it seemed logical enough. After

all, there I'd be, the center of attention with a guy teaching
me all about sex and a sophisticated woman—my sister—
there to give me expert instructions. It would all be like a
kind of advanced course, really not too embarrassing if I
considered it nothing more than a class-room exercise.
And there was, as my sister pointed out, the advantage of
the fact that I wouldn't be getting it from a guy who might
get emotionally involved and I wouldn't g emotionally involved—simply because I was having my first man.

"I guess that all sounds pretty complicate But what I'm
trying to say is simply my sister convinced me it would be
fun if we got this guy up to her apartment and had a sexual
happening where I could learn how it was all done and
how to do it all—without all the emotion complications. I
thought the idea was really appealing.

"I guess every kid wants to find out what is all about in
an easy casual way. I remember thinking how fun it would
be to have it with stranger the first time—some guy I had
never met and would never see again. That way nobody
would know what had happened. I wonder how many
people there are who would like that to happen. And
sometimes I look at people on the street and think how
they all are either screwing or not screwing somebody
else. Then there are the lonely ones who would willingly
get themselves picked up if they thought it was respectable. So many rules against just having a grand old time.
Fun and games!

"Think some night when you're in bed about how
many cocks and pussies are banging it up. It is fantastic
when you think of it that way. So much sex going on. So
many people having orgasms. And all the time, considering the fact that it is night somewhere on the earth all the
time—and people are using the night to screw themselves
silly. All that screwing going on all the time.

"When I think about it, it can make me both sad and
excited. So many girls are taken advantage of—or think

they are and there are so many people hung-up and guilty about their sexual experiences. Then there are all those people who are lonely and don't get their share of the goodies. See what I mean?"

She looked thoughtful for a moment, then lighted a cigarette, and finally continued, saying:

"Well, I got off the point, didn't I? I was telling you about my sister's idea and how it happened that my first man was...well, how it happened.

"I know, telling it this way makes it all sound pretty weird. But it you think about how people sometimes dig threesomes and things like that—some of the things people can do with one another! And then you have the mass orgies. I've gone that scene, too. But I dig it better in private. Though, anything is better than nothing, I guess.

"The conversation between my sister and me had developed so logically that it didn't really seem strange at all. The idea, she suggested. Once we decided what would happen—what we planned on doing, well, it was simply a matter of calling up the stud, so to speak. In fact she called him up right away and made a date. As it turned out it was for the next day—Saturday in the afternoon. Well, I stayed with my sister that night and we talked about what was going to happen and the more we talked the more excited I got.

"When the guy came—he was a looker and built and what a big gun. That was one thing my sister told me. She said: 'This guy's sex organ is really big and powerful. He can do some really wild things with it and can reload pretty fast! Just don't be afraid...a girl can expand to take in that bloated thing like a delicious candy bar if he's got her hot enough. And this stud makes me hot just looking at him. And when he starts doing you with his lips and then...well, all I can say is girlie you're in for one bangin' orgasm! He'll drive you wild, believe me!'

"And he did!

"Boy could he reload that pecker of his. It was large. To my eyes it seemed like a foot long and three inches thick. I don't think I've seen a larger one since. And, of course, I know it wasn't a foot long or three inches thick. But it was large enough and long enough to be more than a mouthful—either mouth. Well, much more than that, actually.

"Guess you know what some guys look like. They come in several different sizes. Small, big, and bigger. The smaller it is the more a girl can service at one time with her lips, the larger the less she can embrace orally. Guess you know what I'm talking about. And another thing!

"It really doesn't make any difference how large a man's cock is. The important thing is how he uses it. A big cock isn't all that important.

"But in this case it was very impressive. And what is more important is that he knew how to use it good and was able to recharge fast enough to be of great use to me.

"My sister and I were undressed and in robes when he arrived and he didn't take long to pull off his clothing and stand between us naked as sin itself.

"We had a short conversation before we disrobed and afterwards. My sister made the introductions and then explained what she had in mind.

"Just came right out and told the truth. You know, that I had an unpopped cherry and was anxious to have to broken in by a skilled lover.

"He dug it plenty! I remember him saying something like, 'That's wild! She's a doll!'

"That thrilled me. And the way he was looking at my body once I pulled off my robe gave me another thrill. He was fairly devouring me with his eyes.

"And his cock started getting big and large just from looking at my titties and … pussy.

"My sister pointed that out casually. Something like 'that's the way you want a man to get affected by looking

110

at you. Big and hard.'

"Well, my sister moved close to—call him Ed—and casually wrapped her fingers around his growing cock, squeezed and then moved them up and down on his prick which was now very big. She flicked a thumb across the crown and said: 'A guy likes this done to him, doesn't he?' Ed grinned and nodded, reaching between her legs and caressing her with the tips of his fingers. 'Just like you dig that!' he announced, cocky as hell. But he had a good reason.

"Just watching was getting me oh so hot. I wanted to masturbate or get into the action.

"I guess my sister realized that because she said for me to touch his cock like she'd done.

"Boy was that fantastic.

"It is something to touch a man's cock for the first time. I was surprised how velvety its flesh was. How hard the shaft. How warm and pulsing. She told me to jerk up and down on it lightly, like I was caressing it. When I did that I felt full of excitement. A thrill.

"It was fun. I wanted to keep it up until it shot off! I love it going off in my mouth, too. That's a real… cock-tail!" She laughed at that, as if it were a joke. Then continued: "Sometimes I've jerked men off, just while they're standing. It is fun. I dig doing all kinds of things. As you might guess from the photos I showed you.

"Anyway, to give you a general idea of what happened, I was told how to caress and squeeze a man's cock and balls. I was shown how a girl can mouth a man's prick. My sister did it first, him lying on the bed. Her head between his legs. She put her lips around his erected shaft and then really took in a mouthful. Slowly she lifted up until her lips were pinching the crown and finally releasing his cock.

"Then she told me to do it.

"Well this guy was getting really orgastic from the

treatment we'd given him to this point.

"When I took her place and put my lips around his cock I was surprised how alive and hot it felt. When it was in a little deeper I thrilled to the feel of it. My sister instructed me to use my tongue, moving it back and forth anyway I wanted to.

"He had fantastic control. He didn't shoot off.

"I mean between the two of us—it might have been difficult for him to keep from creaming one of us. A hot cream cone! Love it. But then…well….

"I don't think I could have handled a come that way. Not the first time.

"Well, in any case, having tried that out, I was told to get up and watch my sister go to work. I guess she was pretty hot to have herself one good orgasm. She straddled his hips and told me to watch and said this was one way to do it with a man. My sister is a fairly aggressive woman, I guess. I can be either way—aggressive or submissive with a man. Just so he comes with a big one.

"Well they really went to town. She pussy-rubbed his prick for a long time, while they frenched each other. When she was ready she inserted his cock into her snatch and went to town!

"She really went at it. Her pussy was really sucking cock. Then she got her orgasm and he'd blown his gun—I'm sure it was a big one! A big fat juicy orgasm for both of them, because they strained like wild and almost passed out afterwards. Then she was off him and caressing his cock, squeezing and molding it into another hard-on. It took a little time, but got hard amazingly fast—as I've learned again since.

"Then she told me to get on the bed with him and then left the room.

"He was smart and expert.

"First he leaned over me and pulled me into arms, just letting me be aware of his nearness. I was learning how a man feels.

"The first time you're against a man like that it is something wild and special.

"I've heard some girls say they'd rather have first sexual session with a guy they cared about. They want it to be a beautiful experience—emotional and love and things like that. I don't agree. At least for me it wasn't that way. The experience I had with Ed was something special because he was a good lover.

"That's the most important thing for a girl. Having a good lover the first time.

"You surely know what I mean. That way it is perfect as it can be. After all, a girl gets hurt when her vagina is bombed out for the first time.

"A gentle lover can make it easier. He can even give her pleasure.

"I don't know what I expected this first time. My sister had told me that it might hurt—of course I knew this...you know how I mean that. After all, my folks had given me quite an education in a general sense. I knew what sex was all about insofar as what was supposed to take place. I'd known for some time. The girls you run around with...they know something—at least some of them. Then my sister had gone through all the details in bloody full-colored detail. I was prepared for the worst. Plus he was so large! Terrifying, really. I figured, well, nothing will be bad after this!

"Of course, as you know, sometimes it doesn't hurt a girl too much. Then, naturally her hymen could be broken by an accident or something like that.

"Any case, I was ready for anything but what actually happened.

"Maybe you've had girls tell you about their first experience with a man. I guess you have."

I nodded and said: "The lucky ones are those who find the experience emotionally and physically satisfying—if not sexually over-whelming."

"Yes. You are right. In my case it was something strangely unexpected.

"Of course, as I've learned since, it wasn't the real big bang. Sex is such a strange thing. It takes time, really, before you are able to know enough to make it really wild. Even then, for the first time around I can't say any more than it was great!

"You see, he held me for some time. He wasn't in a hurry. He knew what he was doing.

"Not all guys know what they are doing. And it is quite an art seducing a virgin—even if it isn't seduction in the sense of convincing her first before you get the goodie. I never really understand why a man wants a virgin. She's so inexperienced."

"Partly ego," I said. "It is taking her innocence for some men—that's the kick. Every man has his own ideas about such things. But I agree with you. Just going out to seduce virgins for the purpose of doing so seems silly. Sex should be something more than that."

"Yes," she agreed with a knowing smile. "You do have a lot of understanding about women."

"Let's say I've learned something about what makes people tick simply by listening."

"Yes. Well, anyway, he kept holding me in his arms and I was highly conscious of the fact that he had a big hard-on pressing against me. Man. Did I! I just keep wondering how I'd ever take that into me! It felt like a brick bat! Yet...oh, so exciting. So hard. And...well...he didn't push things. And he...well...hell...it felt strangely wonderful. I never felt a hard against my naked flesh before. Oh, I'd felt hard-ons while dancing with a guy. You know how kids can dance when they want to be really sexy. Well, a girl can feel a big hard-on against her stomach. Sometimes it is fun to rub your thigh between his legs, against that shaft. I've done that, too, many times. Teasing a man hard, and wondering…well, anyway….

"But feeling it for the first time against my naked flesh was thrilling. And I'd been watching my sister screwing his cock silly. I had never known it could be so exciting watching two making love to one another. Plus, you have to admit, what I'd done orally to his prick had excited me. And I was excited about the whole thing.

"Well, my snatch was getting that way: you know, that hot old feeling that screams for a. man's hard entering and filling it up. Of course I'd never felt a man's prick inside my snatch. But I was ready willing and able.

"I started squirming against him. Quite unconsciously aware of anything but the urge to move…to be sexually more excited.

"Finally he urged me on my back and started caressing me. First, running his hands over my breasts and then along my stomach. It was a wonderful feeling. I forgot all about the fact that this whole thing was happening pretty cold-bloodedly. Well, after all, I didn't even know the guy. The whole purpose was to teach me about love and men and how to be a good lover—under circumstances that would be best for me.

"You know, I've thought since then that everybody should have their first experience this way. Maybe some kind of Government thing. But I guess it would be impossible.

"The thing is that he made love over my body in a beautiful way. He caressed my breasts until the nipples were hurting hard. Then when he kissed my nipples I almost fainted. It felt that good. I don't know if you realize what it does to a woman to have her breasts kissed and sucked I just don't know how to explain it.

A little shiver of excitement moved her.

"It feels so good. And he was good. His tongue circled around the nipples and flicked across them again and again, while his hand was searching over my stomach, across my thighs, circling in light sensual caresses. When his fingers slipped across my snatch—touching the lips for the first time, I tensed all over and a sobbing moan came from my throat. I'd never known anything could feel so delicious and good.

"I was really frantic. I mean he was driving me crazy with sexual excitement. Things were happening to my body that had never happened before.

"I kept remembering what his cock had felt like in my hands and how it had been to have it in my mouth.

"My hand just automatically searched for his hard and found it.

"Boy was he large and firm. Steel. Covered with velvet hot flesh. His balls were tensed tight. I wrapped my fingers around his cock and squeezed, thrilled by the feel of this man thing so aroused and excited by my body. Oh, suddenly I wanted to kiss it and to fill myself with it. I don't know if I wanted it in my mouth or my snatch. I guess I would have taken it in both places at once if that had been possible.

"I kept thinking about what my sister had done with him. And I remembered the orgiastic expressions of pleasure on her face and on his as they were screwing one another.

"And his fingers were now really fondling my snatch and getting real intimate with the lips. When he slipped a probing finger into me I almost came. I was so excited that I almost tore off his bare shaft. My fingers just squeezed real hard around him. I controlled myself only by remembering to be tender to a man's prick. My sister had pointed this out to me.

"I guess he realized I was more than ready. My reactions and then, of course, my snatch was pretty moist, I guess, by then. It should have been. It was raging fire wanting to be fucked royally.

"Hell, I was almost churning against his fingers. I

wanted to be invaded completely.

"He got the message, anyway.

"His body slipped over mine and I swiftly parted my thighs. I parted them really wide. I couldn't wait. Oh, how I wanted it.

"The first contact of his hard shaft against my pussy was so exciting that I simply wiggled up against it.

"I moved back and forth against that hard large cock. Just wiggling and writhing and not knowing exactly what to do. Just being responsive and excited and wanting, so much wanting it in my body. Every nerve was screaming.

"He was a skilled lover and knew how to lead me.

"His hands and his movements told me what to do and suddenly I felt the point of his shaft enter my sexual lips. He didn't immediately attempt to penetrate, but sort of worked the meaty tip around and around, circling my love-lips, opening the doors of my passion wider and wider until I was so aroused and frantic that I made the move. I shoved up against his hard prick, slapping my hips against his. I never knew what hit me. I never felt any pain that I was aware of. Maybe a moment of slight pain—but I don't know. I was so desperate and hot that all I knew was the thrilling awareness of a man's big long shaft penetrating me all the way—right up so deeply I almost felt it would come out my mouth.

"I was simply crazed and clutching him, covering his lips and face with kisses. I couldn't kiss him enough because of the wonderful knowledge of him embedded within my snatch. A part of my body. My first man. My first cock. Oh, I wanted to keep it there forever as some kind of prize!

"He had wonderful control and when he pulled part way out only to plunge slowly back in I almost came. He moved very slowly at first, circling, plunging, lifting, dipping in and out, tugging and pushing my sexual lips with that long big meaty hard shaft of his until I came, all of a sudden had my first real orgasm! He continued to plunge into me again and again after that first come, then as I felt myself gathering another climax he flooded like a fountain deep within me, his shaft convulsing in orgiastic spasms.

"I sobbed and fell back, exhausted and beautifully happy. And I had all his cream inside me, all mine. I wanted to suck his cock. I wanted to go crazy. I was exhausted. It was quite a first experience. It was going to be some years before I really had anything better than that.

"I had other lovers before I moved out of my family's home, like I told you.

"But not until I moved into this place have I had the chance to really swing. It isn't so much that I'm just feeding on sex or want just that. Simply that I have a healthy desire for sexual intercourse with men and this gives me a perfect chance to get my fill without messy emotional problems.

"There are plenty of guys living here that want only sexual kicks and girls like me serve them up because that's what we want. I don't have any desire to get married yet. There is too much living to do. I'm still too young to get all that serious. And there is so much to learn about life before tying myself down to a husband and kids. Once you get married I believe you should know what you want in a sexual partner. You should be willing to settle down completely with that partner. I don't believe in living with a man whom I would share with another woman.

"Well, like my mother and dad. They don't seem to mind. But for me...well, I think that when it gets down to love, I'll be very possessive.

"I don't believe I could enjoy a relationship with a husband who was sharing me with other men.

"In other words, the kind of sex I want right now is casual affairs. When I settle down it will be different. It will be for love. Until that time I believe the thing to do is set myself up in such a way that I can have the kind of social and sexual private life that fulfills my immediate needs. Later will be time enough to get serious and possessive—and until then, I'm going to swing as much as possible.

"Does that answer your questions about my reasons for liking to live in an apartment building like this, 'For Singles Only'?"

I had to admit that she had done a very good job of expressing her views and her motives for living the kind of free-swinging life. Plus she had done a lot to express a general attitude this younger generation seems to have about sex and love and life.

These are not ordinary people, but men and women who live on the cutting edge of the sexual experience. The want to discover anything that might turn them on. They want to experiment. And they are doing just that.

[2005 note: Today such wild explorations can be dangerous, and those who still explore different life-styles, do so with Safe Sex well in mind, or don't last very long in this kind of game.

As always, educational information concerning how to enjoy responsible sexual relations with a partner (or partners) is very important. The idea of refusing to circulate this kind of information is playing with a loaded gun. Ignorance of the facts has never been a smart approach to solving problems.

The moral issues are one thing, but in reality sex is a very strong force in the human experience and anybody responsible enough to enjoy adult relationships should make themselves fully knowledgeable as to the pros and cons involved in such activities.

It is not enough to simply teach our young to say "no!" And, as many people will claim, it is not responsible to have unwanted children. The problems of not letting people decide for themselves concerning birthing, the banning of abortions, can be realistically somewhat of a difficult issue. Over population is a world wide problem which must be faced honestly. Irresponsible sex and unlimited birth is a moral issue for all concerned.

Resolving these issues on a world wide basis is a very serious problem. Pollution is a danger to human existence and vast population centers are vast beds of pollution— over-population caused pollution, and the planet can resist just so much of that kind of torture.

Something will have to give. But just saying "no" and just attempting to control the normal sexual drives of people is simply unrealistic if it isn't done with full information.

It is a problem for all concerned.
And none of it is easily resolved.

Carson Davis

CHAPTER SIX

GINNIE

It takes all types to make up the world and in the world of apartments "for singles only" I had come across quite a few young people searching for a new way of life for themselves. Some were newly breaking away from their homes, trying to discover what it was all about to live in the adult world. They wanted to know the facts, wanted to become a part of something; they were sometimes lonely, sometimes frustrated, but almost always attempting to discover what it was all about.

The world of the late sixties (during which this interview was made) is different from that of the fifties or forties. Things have changed in just about every way. With civil rights being a very real issue of our modern day and with broader understanding of the human race and world history in the making, plus a higher level of education which is far more sophisticated than what many of the earlier generations enjoyed, the young people of today are involved in more than merely a sexual or social revolution. They are not only questioning all the standards handed down to them by their parents, they are beginning to demand answers that are, in many cases, surprising and shocking to others less aware of what is really taking place within the "mind" of man. The collective mind that is searching out not only across the reaches of the earth and space, but across the reaches of the universe, physical and mental. Where yesterday it was frowned upon for men and women to have inter-racial relations, there are those who now seek them out as simply a part of the living experience, no different than any other relationship. Some of these same people are willing to be so broad in their sexual attitude that it will openly embrace homosexual relations as casually as heterosexual.

Such a person is Ginnie. She's attractive, with dark hair cut short, in a modern style. Wears mod dresses and mini skirts, see-through blouses at times, owns a topless bathing suit and works during the day as a secretary for a law firm and a topless dancer now and then at nights, "just for the hell of it!" She was, in my mind, the most interesting person I met at the paradise island, the apartments "for singles only".

Ginnie is full-breasted and has a slim, lovely figure that will make any man turn and look twice. She is strangely more selective than most of the people living in the apartments. This is possibly because of several factors. One being her college education, she has degrees in biology and law. Her business activities at the law firm as a full-time secretary and her "hobby" as a topless dancer.

On the other hand she is far broader in her field of choice—and this could be the reason for her greater selectivity. Plus the fact that she is in her late twenties, been married once for three years, and has a more maturely formed attitude about life. It is not important that another person will agree with her opinions so much as it is a fact that what she had developed into is fairly well-set as a part of her total personality and she is totally adjusted to these sets of values that have become a very great portion of her personality and thought process.

We drank coffee. We sat across from one another in her living room. She had on a short mod skirt and a respectable blouse that made no effort to be sensually seductive. While the other girls I had talked to might easily have become bed partners with me—simply because of the thrill or because it seemed to them a logical thing to do—Ginnie made no indication that such thoughts entered her mind.

The interview was in many ways carried on in almost a computer-like fashion, insofar as any personal interplay between the two of us. She was not unconscious of me as a human being, though at the same time looked upon me as a person gathering facts she willingly gave. Like a lawyer, I might imagine, presenting a case before the jury. Through her way of talking, and the intimate details she was willing to reveal, the honesty of her statements, was as graphic as anyone I have interviewed for these books.

She had requested several of the case history books I've done and read them before our interview. From the minute I walked into her apartment the atmosphere was warm, friendly but at the same time fully business-like. It seemed to be a revealing part of her nature to consider business situations in a serious manner and approach them as such.

Some of her first statements concerning the case history I was putting together on her were the following:

"Life is a serious thing. But there has to be play as well as work."

"Most people don't realize that how they act, what they do, how they relate and react towards others is important not only to themselves but also the other person."

"All relationships are of an emotional nature. No matter how casual. It might be a business matter—such as this immediate one—or it might be an intimate one night stand with a lover, man or woman. But the emotions are there. Nobody can go through a moment of life without thinking and thoughts are loaded with emotional content. Everything you think is motivated by subconscious conditions and attitudes. Nobody can enter into a sexual partnership with another person—even if casual—without feeling something if nothing but sexual desire.

But what makes you have that sexual feeling for the other person? It has to be motivated on an emotional subconscious level. You might not be aware of that consciously, but it has to be. And each relationship will fulfill a different need—or at the least a different shade of a same need. Where a man or woman wishes to be dominated by their sexual partner, each sexual experience will reflect that basic need if it is to be fulfilling. Yet each experience will fulfill the other's immediate personal and psychological needs."

"I don't believe that anything a person can do physically can be morally wrong—as long as those involved are all agreeable and consenting adults. And being adult means, in my book, the ability to take on and handle the responsibilities of one's acts—able to be responsible for the results, no matter what they might be."

"I work very hard during the day. I play hard at night. I try to balance my life in a logical manner so that it is possible to function in a healthy manner at all times. "There are all-too many kids unable to handle the results of their actions. Even here—maybe *especially* here—there are a lot of kids who really don't know what they are doing.

"Look at the animals, if you will. A study of monkeys has shown that they very casually and innocently enter into any kind of sexual activity, homosexual or heterosexual or masturbation. They do what feels good at the time— and don't get all psychologically bothered about it. They enjoy.

"They are simply sliding along without any feeling of responsibility. They are escaping, not really experiencing.

"Marriage and motherhood is a very basic part of life for every woman—as being a father is for men. It is the nature of the human animal. But there is a time and a place for this to happen. And for each person it is at a different time of life. I got married because I wanted to learn what sex was all about. I was too young, inexperienced and foolish. The marriage was a big mistake. It didn't turn me bitter. I merely looked at the ruins, after my divorce went through, and decided that as a human being I had made a bad mistake and if I had anything on the ball, mentally and emotionally, I'd start correcting my attitudes in life to be realistic to the realities of the world. I do want to have children. But that isn't the only human needs I have. I want love. As does every human being. As life stands for me right now I have all the love I need on the level I need it.

"People who believe that homosexual activity is wrong have a big problem. It isn't any more wrong than masturbating. It is simply another way to achieve sexual orgasm.

"I believe that if it were against nature to use means of birth control then we wouldn't have ways to stop conception in the first place. What can be done is perfectly right to do as long as those involved wish to do so.

"Study primitive societies. There are some excellent books that reveal that where children are given total sexual freedom to do anything desire among themselves there is a greater degree of sexual adjustment in adult life and less problems of this nature throughout life.

"Our society is sick, but not because of violence in the streets or because of the so-called sexual revolution, but simply because for generations the Western society has been forced to accept unrealistic attitudes about sex. The moral codes that have been handed down for the last two thousand years are based on what seemed realistic and sane for the societies that originated them—but aren't in our modern world today. Things have changed and people must recognize that.

"I don't believe that when a couple gets married that it is a healthy thing to cheat on one another. It is more honest to swap mates in an open manner. But that is also a sign of a bad marriage. As is the marriage that falls apart because one partner was caught cheating. If a couple can't live through a few rather rough times then their love for one another isn't strong enough. Well, okay, not strong and healthy to begin with.

"I've often wondered that if we had endless lives, promise of immortality in youthful bodies, if it would be possible to love the same mate for eternity. Maybe a hundred years. Maybe a thousand? I doubt that long. For a million or a billion years? No! For eternity? That isn't even realistic. Maybe the idea of immortality isn't realistic—suggested in this sense. But such a question certainly makes one look more seriously at the relationship of love. I believe that people meet and discover a need for one another. It might be for a one night stand. It might be for a prolonged affair. Maybe for several years. Sometimes for several decades. And in some lucky cases for life—which isn't usually for more than something life fifty years at most. What happens when people outgrow their need for one another? Should they stay tied to each other because of marriage vows? Or should they part company in a friendly manner?

"I realize that the relationship between man and wife—or mates, if you wish—can become highly involved to a degree where the sexual thing is of little importance against what each has grown to mean to the other over the years. They still enjoy the sexual love and it becomes a more meaningful thing to them when experienced and shared together; but there is far more to their relationship—and that is a mutual growing together, becoming a unit, almost perfectly meshed. This is, naturally, the ideal real love-partnership. It doesn't happen all that often, sadly enough. Because we are all human beings. Sometimes each person in the marriage partnership grows in opposite directions after a period of time—be that a few years or a few decades.

"To stay static is to be frozen in some kind of psychological mind-trap where you aren't growing in a healthy way, but rather merely rotting—existing.

"In other words to get the most out of life we must, in order to survive, grow from each and every experience. We should not be the same person today that we were yesterday—and tomorrow we must be changed just that little bit more to be able to say the same thing. Change is the very nature of the universe. Nothing stays the same. There is movement. Where there is no movement we have a void.

"As I don't believe there is anything wrong in experiencing homosexual relationship—if such seems right at the time—nor do I believe there is anything wrong with inter-racial relationships. I've experienced both with a great deal of pleasure. I have in every case related to the person—human being, personality—involved in such acts with me.

"In the same manner I have discovered there is nothing wrong with mass orgies—if you wish to call them that. Sexual situations where more than two people are involved with one another. Call it the sex circus. As long as all are responsible adults and consenting and enjoying what they do in private."

All this was stated very much like a computer spitting out information. There was humor in some of her statements. At times her eyes flashed with slight irritation or anger, though, beyond that, Ginnie went through these basically opening statements much as a lawyer might make an opening statement before a jury. To her they were facts of life and totally accepted and really not open to argument—though she didn't expect everybody to accept her conclusions as their own moral attitude. Nonetheless she was simply putting forth in a rapid manner what she considered to be her own personal code and one which she believed to be realistic and ethical.

Before any actual exchange started she made this very point clear by saying: "Nobody has a right to tell me what I do is wrong except myself, if for no other reason than I'm willing to accept the results of my acts. I've found that for me this is the best way in which to live a happy, fulfilling life. I do not really expect others to openly embrace my attitudes, though I expect them to respect my rights to have them. I don't make any attempt to force my beliefs on others and I expect the same from others concerning my feelings. Like religion, each person must make up their own mind and have the freedom to do so. That is one of the basic rights that our nation was supposed to be built on."

At this point Ginnie took a break in order to offer me more coffee, which I accepted. We lighted cigarettes, relaxed a few moments and then she asked what I thought of her attitude and what she'd told me.

I said: "If for no other reason other than the 'disclaimer' you tagged onto the end, I couldn't find fault with what you say. As to each and every point, I do feel that for many people it would be impossible to accept them in body without at least some minor changes here and there."

She grinned at that and announced: "You certainly ride down the middle and don't give out any roses."

"My position is that I'm here to listen, to ask certain questions and get what answers you wish to give. I'm not here to attack your attitudes or rip them apart.

"But," she pointed out with another generous smile, "you'll have the last word when you put all this down on paper."

"That, too, is part of my job. But I try to be fair."

"I noticed that in your books. You've only entered into things when the person needed help—and you've always suggested they seek professional help. That's smart in every way. I have to admire the way you handle people.

That's why I was willing to give you this interview. It seemed like a means to express my views and maybe as a result reach some people who might see something in them that could be helpful. If I'd felt you would distort my statements I wouldn't have been willing to sit still for it."

"I'll go even further than that," I offered. "If you wish, I'll let you look over the final draft and make any corrections or changes you wish to make."

She shrugged. "I have a feeling about people. I feel you are honest and that you will report what I say in the manner in which I say it. If you wish to show me the final draft I'll look it over only for the purpose of seeing if I did express myself clearly. It isn't necessary as far as I'm concerned."

As it turned out, though, I did let her see the final draft of the transcript itself and she was very helpful in making certain suggestions. I had marked which portions I planned on using and pointed out what my own statements would be. It wasn't necessary to go beyond that.

In any case the bulk of the interview went as follows:

"Tell me," Ginnie inquired, "where from your point of view should I start?"

"Usually I let people talk—even if ramblingly—and later edit and arrange the conversation in a logical manner so as to make their points as clear as possible."

She nodded, lighted another cigarette, leaned back in the padded chair, threw her feet up on the foot stool in front of her and then after breathing out smoke between pursed lips, she said: "Ever since hearing about your project and then looking at your books I've wondered just what I wanted to say. How much I was willing to reveal. Until you came I still didn't know for sure how much detail it would be possible to give. I've always felt that a person's sexual life is private. But in the immediate case I feel that my true identity is to be kept hidden, and since the best way to tell my story—and make my points—

would probably be by detailed illustrations of some of the things that have happened to me, it doesn't seem like a very hard thing to do.

"Then, of course, I would imagine that all of us human beings, one time for another would like to strip aside all the social niceties and come down to blunt, basic terms, revealing all the details of our sexual experiences. Psychologically it makes sense. A kind of mental house cleaning. In fact, like just about every person, I've used all the dirty words in the English language—when the moment seemed right. The idea of using them in one great big mental bowel movement certainly can't have anything but a healthy result."

She laughed lightly and then added: "Plus, to make people really know how it is you have to be graphic and tell it in terms that makes the most impressive reaction. If you say I was with the Negro and he made love to me and it was a beautiful experience, nobody is going to really feel the experience like I did. If I say that making it with a Lesbian was a delightful revelation in sexual responses it won't cause anybody to really know how important this event was or why it was so impressive. At least, that's the way I feel about it."

"The important thing is to simply tell what you wish in the manner you believe most effective, or desirable," I suggested.

"Like I told you I was married and a virgin on the wedding night. I see no reason to go into that relationship simply because it was all a mistake. The only thing I would like to point out is that a woman is a damned fool to take the chance of getting married to a man she hasn't at least slept with once—and she's smarter to have an affair with him first! I'm not saying the marriage won't succeed. That would be foolish. Too many marriages succeed even when both man and woman are virgins on their wedding night. But I've seen a good argument against waiting until wedding bells have sounded before learning what sex is all about. I don't mean simply my own big mistake. Forgetting that. The law firm I work for has handled a lot of divorce cases and all too many of these are caused because two people got married too young with far too little sexual experience. I've known more couples who had successful marriages that slept with one another before marriage than I know successful marriages where they didn't.

"Like you pointed out in at least one of your books: get sex out of the way first! I learned that the hard way and I've seen since then one hell of a lot of examples to prove it a very sane attitude. Still, everybody has to do what they think is best. For myself I would advise a daughter or sister or girl friend to make things as easy as possible once the marriage has come into being. There are enough problems not to add to them. When two people start living together they have a lot of adjustments to make—the less to face after the marriage the better chances of success. If they got married just to have sex—because they didn't feel they should outside of the marriage relationship—chances are the only thing going for them is sex. Not always true, naturally. Even then, though, there's a lot of failures. Some say that living together dulls the relationship and it falls apart. Keeping some things a mystery until the wedding night, they claim, is just down right smart. Hell, I say, no matter what you do before marriage, there are going to be unlimited surprises, and not all of them enjoyable!

"But as for me, when I get married the next time it will be with everything well worked out before hand and there won't be any of this jumping into such a serious stage of human relationship until I've solved all those problems possible to solve. I believe the best thing for people to do is to live together for a year or two. Then they have a chance to not only have sex out of the way but also know a little about one another's living habits on a daily basis.

"So enough of the marriage routine. Other than to say

you can't own another person—and you can't have something which isn't freely given. Well, anyway....

"We divorced. I settled back to figure out what had happened. For a few months I didn't date. When I did start dating I knew what I was after in my relations with men. I had read a lot and learned a lot about what makes people tick. I talked to a psychologist friend of mine. By the time I started dating I was ready to accept myself as a sexual creature who would relate to people around me in a total manner—no matter how involved that might be. Or how casual. I wouldn't sleep with every man I met. On the other hand if it seemed right to go to bed with them the first night out—that was what would happen. Some times saying 'no' is as perverse as saying 'yes' at the wrong time!

"On the point of dating. I had come to the conclusion and realization that a man and woman will usually seek out each other's company because there is a sexual feeling between them. Just like when a man sees a pretty girl who attracts him enough to make an effort to take her out—because he actually would find it highly exciting to sleep with her—so a woman, if she is really honest and mature about herself, usually dates only those men she would find exciting to climb into bed with. What each of us do in this society is lie to ourselves. Plus, there are some women who will date men simply to use them and be escorted. For myself I don't have the time for that.

"And, without trying to brag, the fact remains that I have the kind of looks that a good number of men find attractive and make an effort to package what nature gave me in a way that will be even more attractive. Thus I do find myself in a position where it isn't all that hard to obtain male companionship. Because of this I have no difficulty in picking the kind of man who excites me. There are some girls—and men, of course—who aren't that lucky and they have to take what is offered. I'm lucky.

"By the time I was ready to date I had the chance to go out with an older man who I found extremely attractive. He erotically excited me.

"I was working as a secretary in another law firm—part of the secretary pool—and he was one of the clients. I just happened to be doing work for the man who had his account. One day he came up to my desk and asked if I would have dinner with him. The time was right. I'd come to the conclusion that I would very soon be ready to date. His offer was readily accepted. When I'd seen him in the lawyer's office, while delivering some legal papers I'd typed, it had been pretty difficult to ignore his sensual maturity. The tall, firm build, the sensitive, but sexy eyes and the friendly, confident turn of his lips when he smiled. That first look made me think that here was a man a girl like me could go for.

"The date offered and accepted meant to me a sexual affair. I wanted to be seduced by him.

"I won't go into the details of the date. It isn't important. He drove me to my apartment. I invited him up for a nightcap. He accepted with the full knowledge of what I was offering. It was a mature, open, honest and casual thing.

"I'd told him about my marriage and during the evening the conversation had naturally turned to sensual topics and I'd never once attempted to indicate anything other than my being as interested in him as a man as he admitted to being interested in me as a woman.

"Once in the apartment I told him where the drinks were, excused myself, went into my bedroom, got undressed and picked out my most revealing nightie.

"When I returned to the living room he had cocktails waiting on the coffee table and was sitting on the sofa. Neither by act or expression did he indicate anything but open pleasure and delight in my offering. His whole attitude was respectful acceptance of what we were going to do and pleasure in my honesty in not playing childishly foolish coy games.

"I sat down next to him and he commented on how lovely and desirable I looked while handing me one of the highballs.

"He placed an arm around my shoulders, gently leading me against him in a very friendly, natural way. We sat, sipped our drinks and talked generally about ourselves. As the drinks emptied the conversation became more personal. He began saying nice, lovely things to me. It was a romantic situation, not a crude sexual meeting. His voice was husky with emotion when he said how lovely my eyes and lips and face and shoulders were. He admired my figure and said how beautiful I looked. We were relating as two human beings, knowing what each needed and wanted and willing to give it.

"His attitude was acceptance of my gift of love and he respected it as such--not a taking as so many men believe it to be. The woman gives herself and in case men don't know it this is the greatest gift she can give a man—even if given in a casual manner. He was mature and sophisticated enough to realize this.

"By the time the drinks were finished he took my glass and lay it on the sofa and then pulled me slowly into his arms. We kissed gently at first. His lips caressed my eyes and cheeks and nose and then covered my mouth. His hands gently pulled me firmly close and then as our tongues moved against one another in erotic kisses, I felt one hand slip under the top piece of my nightie and caressingly move up over my breast, gently fondling. The kiss lasted long enough to build the basic sexual needs within both of us. Then he slowly gathered me up in his arms, stood and carried me into the bedroom, kissing my eyes and lips and cheeks and throat, while saying how lovely I was.

"He knew that as a woman I needed to be loved in a

way that would make me feel secure emotionally. Any person who goes through a divorce usually needs to be convinced that they are sexually desirable and haven't failed on this level in their relationship with their marriage partner.

"This man realized how much a woman in my position needed love of a more tender and meaningful kind.

"Not emotional love but romantic love. Not a demanding thing, or a taking thing, but a pure giving act of mutual joy of love.

"I remember being placed on the bed. My eyes were closed and I wanted this lover to join me. It didn't seem really very long.

"I heard the sound of clothing rustling. I heard movement. Then I felt weight press down on the bed and he was lying beside me.

"He tenderly pulled me into his arms and made over me for some time with words and kisses and finally caresses, running his hands over my body and breasts and stomach. Several times he lowered his caress until he reached between my thighs and slowly slipped upwards to lightly stimulate my vagina. Once he slipped his fingers under my panties to give me the first naked caress. I was thrilled and excited, totally aroused by this time.

"Then I remember he glided the top of my nightie up over my breasts, exposing them to naked caresses and finally erotic, voluptuous tongue kisses. By then I was so aroused that I was on the point of desperation. A good lover will know when to move and he knew. I was already aware of the largeness of his hard shaft against my thigh and when he started to peel down my panties I lifted up my hips to help. He caressed the cloth away and then rolled over on top of me, his hard shaft finding a natural place against the lips of my vagina. I didn't want to wait this first time and he sensed this. Almost immediately he penetrated me and my legs wrapped about his, gripping body to me in orgiastic pleasure. I am sure I experienced a climax in the first moments of intercourse. His shaft was very large and hard as it worked in and out with controlled skill. It continued to enter and re-enter me time and again until I experienced another climax just as he reached the point of orgasm. I had a multiple orgasm as a result. Only after he had left me and slid alongside my body could I fully relax in the aftermath of his love-making.

"Though it wasn't long before both of us were sexually active again. But this time I became a mutual partner, caressing his penis until it was hard and finally discovering it was impossible to keep from kissing this hard shaft and then folding my lips around its crown. He gripped my thighs and lifted my hips, turning me around so that I was straddling his lips, at which time he began loving me orally, too.

"I guess we made love two more times before falling asleep in each other's arms. The next morning we made love again. He left a little before noon, after having breakfast and making me promise to give him another date.

"We went out a couple of more times and then he had to leave town on business. By that time I met some other men I found interesting and started dating them."

She paused and then smilingly said: "I don't think I mentioned it, but he was a light skinned Negro. I would have never thought it would be possible to have interracial relations until the moment he stepped up to my desk and asked me out. I wouldn't have imagined it could be such a wonderful and lovely experience with any man as it was with him."

I asked: "You had planned from the first to let him make love to you?"

"I had accepted the fact that I wouldn't date any man I wouldn't be willing to sleep with. I didn't know if it would happen, but I was willing to let it, if things worked out that way.

136

"You don't think you did it for kicks?"

"Are you kidding? And even if I had—it certainly didn't turn out that way. I've had plenty of chances to sleep with Blacks just for kicks, but won't. I seldom have sexual relations merely for kicks. If it happens that way it is because it seems the most natural thing.

"I've been at some of these parties they give here at the apartment and ended up as naked as the others, reaching out for whatever is nearby.

"I've gang-banged because at the time it seemed like a fun idea. That happened not too long ago.

"Three guys were sitting at the pool, I came down in a bikini and we all got to talking. Each had seen me naked at parties and having sexual relations at such parties. We started talking and ended up going to my apartment for drinks and getting naked. I lay on the bed and let the first one enter my vagina while I played with the other two, one on each side. As the one screwing me fast and rapid built to climax I had the other two hard as rocks. The first left and one of the others took his place. I squeezed and fondled and played with the guy who had climaxed in my vagina, getting him ready for a second round. I climaxed fantastically with the second guy and when the first climbed on, entering into intercourse with me I climaxed almost immediately again. Before we were finished, each man had entered me at least twice. One a third time. For some reason it seemed like an exciting thing to do and I enjoyed every moment of it.

"As for women lovers, I've learned it can be very good with a Lesbian. Though it is not my greatest bag.

"A girl friend of mine was rooming with a bisexual and one night I went over to visit them. We talked about sex and this bisexual girl started saying she got some real kicks with Lesbians. I never had any relations with her, but it set me up for what happened several months later. One woman who worked at the same company I did was a

Lesbian, but one of those very attractive, baby-doll women. You would never think she was anything but a normal, wild, healthy girl. We became friends. One day she suggested I come over and have dinner with her. Since I didn't have anything planned for that night I accepted. I didn't know what she had in mind.

"Once at her place she served martinis, had romantic music on and let the conversation slowly get around to sex. It isn't hard for conversations to develop into a sexual exchange.

"I was feeling my drinks and this girl was very nice and a good companion. She had a bright brain and was able to make a conversation light and entertaining. Before we had finished the meal she admitted to having had sexual relations with women. I don't really remember how it all came up to that point, but it all developed very naturally. I remember talking about the bisexual girl I'd met and she started telling me the pleasures of Lesbian love.

"Before I knew it she was showing me a dildo. I'd heard there were such things—somewhere along the line. But I didn't realize I'd ever see one or that it would seem so realistic. Even a moveable foreskin! It was padded by a kind of foam rubber. She explained that when a girl used this on another girl it could really be something special. She even had a device to strap it between her legs so that it could be used by her in the same fashion as a man would use his penis on a woman.

"I was fascinated by the thing.

"I really don't know what caused me to go along with the idea. But it happened. I can only say that it was rather interesting feeling a woman's breasts against my own. She was a skilled lover. She had told me that a girl knew better how to excite another female, because she knew where to start first and where to end.

"She had told me of some of her own erotic experiences and how one girl had used a dildo in her rear and how much pleasure it had given. 'With a man, I've been told, it can't possibly last so long. If your lover is good she can make the dildo give you more orgasms than you can count!' was her promise.

"I was pretty drunk, in any case. So when we were naked on the bed and she started loving me up, I responded sexually. She was very good at cunnilingus. I don't believe I've known anybody who was better at it. She knew how to kiss a woman's breasts in the most erotic way—as good as the best of male lovers. Some men can be a little rough.

"When she started really working me over with the dildo—which was strapped to her waist so it dangled between her legs like a man's hard penis, I got terribly orgasmic. By the time she inserted the thing into me I was ready to come. She kept it up for such a long time, never stopping. First moving in a slow, circular penetration, and then speeding up as she saw I was coming; then she started the slower movements until I was reaching for another climax. She knew exactly when to change the rhythm. She kept it up beyond the point where I thought I could take another climax. That last orgasm ripped through my body with such voluptuousness that I lost consciousness afterwards."

"How'd you feel about what had happened, later?" I inquired when she paused for a moment.

"Not guilty if that's what you mean. I merely accepted it as another way to sexual orgasm. I accepted the experience the same way I accepted the first time I had two men in bed with me at once.

"That was really something. I'd never experienced possession of two erected—well, cocks. They were cock artists. Brothers. Having one to feed upon and another which my vagina could work with was strangely overwhelming. It is an experience. I'll tell you!

"Just like the first time I experienced anal intercourse. That was after the Lesbian thing. That night the girl had talked me into letting her use the dildo on me that way. It was pretty good. I'd never realized I was sensitive there.

"So one night when a man asked if I'd ever had anal intercourse I found the idea highly appealing. I was very interested in knowing how different the experience might be with a man's real penis penetrating me in this manner. It was quite different. I could feel his quite alive reactions. His shaft had a life that responded almost pulsingly to me. Then there were the sounds of his own pleasure that added to the experience. Of course, he was able to have an orgasm while the dildo naturally couldn't."

"When you were with the Lesbian did you make love to her or use the dildo?"

"Yes. But with my hands, as an experiment," she admitted quite evenly. "It didn't do much for me, but it was kind of a way to return what she'd given my body. You can't just take pleasure without trying to return it. Too many lovers act like that. I don't like men who are that way.

"Once I was with a guy who wouldn't let me fondle him or orally stimulate his penis. It irritated me quite a bit. I enjoy doing things like that, too. But there are all kinds of lovers."

"What is it that you find desirable about living in this apartment for singles only?" I inquired after a long pause in the conversation.

"Probably different from some of the other answers you have heard. Maybe not. But I'm not doing it because it makes things particularly easier for me. Getting lovers, that is. I don't believe in climbing into bed with every male I meet. On the other hand if things seem right I certainly won't turn down a good pleasure session. I think it is just as wrong to turn away from a sexual experience as it is to jump into bed with each and every offer made.

"Some of the people here want sex without the effort it takes to create a kind of personal relationship. They want

140

things the easy way and believe this is the only easy way. I never find it difficult to get a lover. I'm not bragging. It is simply a fact of life that any woman who is even the least bit attractive and makes an effort to show herself off in public in an attractive package can get a man with little effort. Beyond that, she'll probably know quite a few men who are willing to be invited over for the night.

"If you'll notice some girls when they go to a bar that is basically a pick-up place, they'll gather together at a table and talk. They feel more comfortable with other girls around. If a woman is mature and sophisticated and wants to be picked up by a mature man all she has to do is go into a nice high class cocktail lounge, sit at a table by herself casually look around. It isn't long before some man will get the message you're on the make, so to speak. Though I don't find this necessary I've discovered such things happening by accident. Only once did I take up such an offer.

"You see, many times I'll stop off at a bar after work—a nice high class place—and have a cocktail. Usually I'm exhausted and want to relax alone. Countless times a man has come up offering to give me company and conversation and a drink and hopefully a big sexual thrill in some hotel room. I've politely turned them down. Once I found the guy so exciting that I allowed the conversation to lead to a free drink and finally we left the place together. But, as it turned out, he was the kind of man who interested me not only physically but personally. We did more than a one night stand. I dated him for quite a few months and we are still fairly good friends, though we have passed the affair stage. We're just friends, now.

"That kind of thing can happen where you meet a stranger in a cocktail lounge and you become lovers and then friends. But usually that's not the case.

"So what I'm trying to say is that I don't need this kind of set up because it makes it easy to get lovers. In fact if anything I'm less of a swinger than most around here. It isn't my purpose...easy sexual relations. I like living here simply because it is a place for young people with young ideas and living the kind of social life that can make my own more fulfilling. They are for the most part a nice bunch of people. Some mixed up and some floundering. But generally a lot more fun than people who usually live in apartments—put another way, most apartments rent to married couples, some singles—and all ages.

"Here we have something in common, and are all eager to be friendly. You don't have the problem of being called up on the phone by the manager saying you're making too much noise. You can live the kind of life you want without problems. Everybody gives and takes a little. It has to do, I guess, with the fact that it is better to be living in a situation which gives you enough freedom to live a privately rewarding and fulfilling life and at the same time be on friendly and social terms with the people living around you—people your own age with interests that come closer to matching your own.

"Sure there are a lot of wild parties, but it is all in privacy. Only those who wish to come are there and they know what to expect. They are all consenting adults. At least in the legal sense. Nobody is forced to do anything they don't want to do.

"And believe me there aren't all that many wild parties. Usually they aren't much different from parties given all around the nation by all age groups.

"A hell of a lot of married couples living in the suburbs have wild parties, swap partners, have mass orgies—gang bangs. You name it and its being done.

"We're single, free and mature. We have no real responsibilities to anybody but ourselves."

She paused and then said: "Well, to say it in a simple way : it makes things easier for everybody this way. That's reason enough for such an arrangement as this."

142

Thus ended the basic portion of the interview with Ginnie. The rest of the conversation was light, general and had little to do with the subject of this book.

* * * * * * *

In conclusion I would like to say that while I interviewed other members of the apartment, none revealed much more other than collectively offering a general attitude that I feel would be of interest to.

Generally most of the men and women I talked to felt that living in this kind of apartment solved some of the problems that people a decade before had when going out on their own.

One girl said this: "When my brother—he's ten years older than me—moved away from home, he complained that it was really difficult to get to meet girls his own age. He didn't like going to pick-up joints but finally was forced to do this in order to meet girls. The problem is that once you are out of school and you're still single and no serious involvements with a member of the opposite sex you find yourself cut off. You're in the world of adults and it is difficult to find people your own age with the same interests you have. This apartment and places like it solve the problem for the most part. We get a chance to meet people our own age. We don't have the problem that men and women over thirty had when they were our age. And since we're a little more open about sex now days we have perhaps a fuller and freer sexual experience all the way around. That's what makes these kinds of apartments so important!"

Her statement made me realize how it was when I left school and what my own feelings were and those of my friends.

At one point we were surrounded by people our own age, the next day we were isolated. There weren't any easy meeting places. You had to hope there would be people who knew girls that might be interesting and interested in dating you. The pick was limited. You could go to pick-up bars, but not everybody wanted this kind of relationship with the opposite sex. And since it made it harder to meet people of the opposite sex one was easily moved into marrying somebody who might not prove to be a perfect marital partner for them.

This situation still exists for most young people. It probably always will for many if not most. But the apartments for singles only are just one answer to the social problem of meeting unmarried men and women with the same basic social interests.

It is surely not everybody's answer. Some people would find such a "social" arrangement undesirable simply because their personal moral ethics would not allow them to become involved in what they consider casual sexual relations.

But what is good for one is not always good for another. It takes a lot of different kinds of people to make up the world and a lot of different kinds of social situations to make these people happy.

If all the people had been like those mentioned in this book, I would have to conclude that these apartments are maybe a little too "wild"; but for the most part the kids living there were nice, average young people seeking the meaning of life—sometimes through sexual affairs of a serious nature, some like those in this book who revealed the "swinger" and "groover" or like Ginnie, the girl—and man—who want a certain kind of single life—aren't planning on getting married—and demand that their sexual experiences be given the total freedom they desire in order to fulfill their living experience.

All, in time, probably got married and had children. They are a part of the vast generation that took over the responsibilities of industry, business and government of the nation. What will be their attitudes when their children mature into young adults? Will they have the same open-minded attitude their parents seem to be having today, or will they reverse and make a round about turn and attempt to bring a more restrictive social form into existence?

Well their children are today's mainstream! And a few are just as interesting is discovering their own, personal pathway to greater understanding of their sexual, sensual sides. And exploring the very meaning of their lives in new ways.

In fact, since the above case history was originally taped and later published, a few decades have passed, experimental living styles haven't lost their fashion. Instead of apartments made for singles only, there are groups of people who get together to explore all kinds of inter-relationships. Every generation brings their own take to such things. One man who was introduced to me by a mutual friend offered to sit down and let me let me record our conversation, which is, in part, offered as a closer. He wouldn't like me to call him a guru, or even a leader, yet he has a group which is loosely connected insofar as living arrangements are concerned—not living in a mutually shared apartment house for singles only, but rather coming together for group gatherings, even therapy sessions that involve a multiple of what some would call "sexual exercises."

He had this to say, especially after having read some of the *Swingles* case histories:

"My experience feels very individual" he pointed out, somewhat carefully. Almost guarded. "Even though I hang out with others that might be perceived as on the 'cutting edge', we are all very different, and I've pursued my cutting edge independently of others. My impression of the alternative sexuality crowd is that the only thing they have in common is an acceptance of whatever someone needs to do to get off, whatever their kink is. You go to a BDSM scene, and people are into a dozen different things; tickling, whipping, hanging, binding, dripping hot wax, exposure, needlework, clothing, on and on—yet most people there only have one or two things that actually turn them on."

"And you? Where do you personally draw the line, so to speak?"

"As far on 'the edge' that I am, I don't like swinging, or bondage, or sadism/masochism/pain—a tiny bit of dom/sub, but not the way I see others do it. I'm not into bisexuality, although I'm comfortable with it and have done my dabbling; and I have some kinks that very few others are into.

"I don't seem to like group scenes unless they are people emotionally connected with me. I've done them, but I don't seek them out. On the other hand, I've found several things that are thrilling, and I love repeating them, and I miss them when I don't do them—group cuddling, group sexual massage, watching or being watched making love, a threesome with two people I care about, silly and childish sexual play, tickling."

"But, from what you've told me in the past, you've been in to some different kinds of things." I knew he was into poly sex, where one might bond to more than a single sexual partner, but in a more serious way than merely swinging. "Come on, sock it to me!"

"Ok, Carson, I'll go out on a limb here."

"Limbs can always be useful, keep you from fall on you behind." I said with some humor.

He nodded seriously at that, then said: "An example is I have a pee fetish. I get turned on watching a woman pee."

He paused, perhaps for dramatic effect. I asked: "And…what to tell me what and why you enjoy this?"

"I can't explain it, it makes no sense, but it's definitely there."

Again a pause, so I inquired: "You almost sound like you are uncomfortable about this. Don't let me bother you, or the fact this will be published. You're name will remain totally unknown to the world at large." I had to laugh at that, cause he wasn't the kind of man who would really be uncomfortable. And in fact he assured me that wasn't the case. And he also went out of his way to underscore he attitude about what it was sharing.

"It's not dirty to me—but it is 'naughty', forbidden, shocking, and that adds to the thrill."

"Okay. Shouldn't be. We all have our special secret pleasures. Nothing alarming nor naughty about that!"

"It is actually a fairly common fetish, although not as well known as bondage, for example; yet I know very few people into it, and the women I have convinced to do it do it to please me, not because it turns them on. But at a festival celebrating kinky sexuality, I could do a workshop on 'watersports', and get a lot of curious people who would not be judgmental, and maybe a couple of people who were actually into it."

"Yes, you'd told me about some of the workshop's you have run." He was a kind of self-made guru to a number of people who valued his guidance. "Your own group seems to be very experimental and open to new things and self-discovery, not only in sexual experiences, but in many others. They are mutually sharing adults seeking an expanded experience, somewhat different from the standard one out culture seems to favor, marriage, kids, family, etc. You appeal to these people who want to stretch their boundaries in a number of ways. Right?"

He nodded and then continued rather thoughtfully:

"It is a world where everyone understand and respects each other's need and right to explore their sexuality as they need to. If someone is into squirting whip cream up their butt, everyone would say, well, that's not for me, but if it gets them off, the more power to them—and they would be accepted on the basis that they are willing to explore their own unique passions, rather than stay stuck in mundane sexuality."

"Tell me a little about your group! The types of people, what they're into."

"There are those who find their niche—swinging, bondage, orgies, polyamory, whatever—but many people get bored with one form after a while and move on to something else. The thrill of doing the forbidden does not last forever when it is no longer forbidden. But the basic drive to explore one's sexuality wherever it leads seems to be a common thread."

"Of course, we're all trying to find a new way to understand ourselves and experience life in a new fashion. And as you say, anything can become, swiftly, old hat. What is your own sense...how do you feel? In your own path is the group a major item of business for you or only part of what you seek? Or are you more of a loner at heart?"

"My feeling is that I forge ahead alone—I have support in the sense of others consider my journey legitimate, even exciting, and are willing to follow where I lead—but I find my desire leads in a slightly different path than others, so I still have the feel that I am doing something new and uncharted, even though plenty of others have done things just as brave."

"That's important to you, right? This...how do you call it?"

"It's not just the quest to understand sexuality; it's the quest to understand my unique set of desires and quirks, to see where they lead, to wonder what they are about, and to enjoy the unique pleasure that comes from them."

What makes his ideas especially interesting is that he does have a group of people who come to him, and to a great extent is their "leader"—or, at least, someone they admire enough to listen to. I didn't get the impression he's on an ego trip, but merely a search.

And much like the Swingles of a few decades back, this man is continuing a kind of universal search every people goes on to some extend, some more boldly than others, but it takes place in ever generation.

It will be interesting to see the results. Whatever they might be, whatever the direction taken in the next twenty or so years, let us all hope that it will be for the best of humanity and civilization on this planet we call Earth.

ABOUT THE AUTHOR

Carson Davis is just another pen name for a rather pro-lific writer who had many other pen names and scores of books published during his writing career.

The author reports that when he started writing his agent told him that the really hungry market for beginning writers was the so-called "adult novels" aimed at male sexual fantasies. This market, over the years, changed dramatically. When his publishers started releasing case-history books he created the Carson Davis name, which appeared on some twenty pocketbooks.

Now Wildside Press is offering a few of Mr. Davis' books to its readership. The realistic grounding of his work is starkly evident. And his continual message reflects a non-judgmental attitude about people's moral ethics.

He writes:

"I have lived in Southern California most of my life, and perhaps that has molded my own personal convictions concerning morality. I've experienced marriage in a won-derful way. And like "Carson Davis" I've been convinced that real love and commitment comes when people are willing to share their lives together in an honest and lov-ing manner. How that shapes itself is a matter of each per-son's beliefs and standards.

"These books, under the Carson Davis byline, have always been an especially rewarding experiment, for they

gave me a chance to express a lot of basic thoughts and ideas which can't be articulated in straight novels in exactly the same way. In the case history format I was able to examine ideas and concepts that reached across many cultural and religious borders. The only restriction was the theme of each book. Beyond that I could do pretty much what seemed most reasonable.

"I didn't depend only on my own knowledge concerning human sexology, but drew upon the excellent advice of a minister and therapist willing to share solid information dealing with the thematic material all of these books covered. Because of this I have felt they offered very important truths about life, sex, relationships and some essential insights into a wide array of thinking concerning the human condition..

"I have never talked to a person who was a real pervert or deviant, but rather to many people with different points of view who had something to reveal in their apparent "confessions" about life, sex and what they believed was the ideal solution to just surviving.

"It is enough to say these books were popular and have found circulation throughout the world. They stand up today as well as they did when originally published."

www.ingramcontent.com/pod-product-compliance
Lightning Source LLC
Chambersburg PA
CBHW051924240626
47153CB00004B/1353